ST. PAUL'S SCHOOL LIB…
LONSDALE ROAD, SW13 9JT
KT-160-702

VOICES FROM THE PLAINS

John Colet
ST. PAUL'S SCHOOL
LIBRARY

ST. PAUL'S SCHOOL LIBRARY
LONSDALE ROAD, SW13 9JT

VOICES FROM THE PLAINS

GIANNI CELATI

Translated by Robert Lumley

Contents

To those who told me stories, many of which are transcribed here.

The island out in the Atlantic

I have heard a story told about a radio ham from Gallarate, in the province of Varese, who made contact with someone who lived on an island out in the Atlantic. The two of them used to communicate in English, a language the Italian radio ham didn't understand very well. However, he realized that the other man always wanted to describe the place where he lived — to tell him about the coastline beaten by waves, the sky that was often clear even when it was raining, the rain that came down horizontally on the island because of the wind, and about the things he could see from his window.

The Italian radio ham, in order to understand more of what was said, began to record their conversations and get his girlfriend to translate the tapes, since she knew English better than he did.

The man only wanted to talk to him about the island. With him, the radio ham never managed to have the normal exchange of technical information or news of other radio hams dotted around the world. And when occasionally he tried to ask him who he was, what he did, and whether he'd been born there or was a newcomer, the man evaded his questions as if he didn't want to hear them. The only thing about him that the young man from Gallarate had found out was that he was called Archie, that he lived with his wife, and that every day he used to take long walks around the island.

Listening over and over again to the tape-recordings and talking about them with his girlfriend, the radio ham gradually began to picture the island as if he had seen it with his own eyes.

It was as if he could see it out there, stretching, concave, beneath Archie's house which stood on a promontory. A road made a long curve through fields where sheep and cows grazed on open ground, and to the right there was a lowish headland entirely covered in heather. On the left, he could see a rocky coastline, broken up here and there by beaches that rose steeply from the sea, leading up to a small plateau that blocked out the horizon; and, over there, you could just make out a few scattered farms.

Looking to the left, out to sea, it seemed on clear days that you could follow the curve of the earth as far as the blurred shape of a lighthouse which was, according to Archie, the most westerly point of the mainland where it reached out into the Atlantic.

Even the name of the island was never mentioned by Archie, though he would always tell him about his walks, taking many features of the place for granted as if the young man from Gallarate lived next door. But was there a house next door? And did that island exist?

One day the radio ham was playing back a tape with his girlfriend and, after listening to one of the usual descriptions of the place, heard the following words spoken by Archie in a hushed voice: 'I'll never see any of this again.'

By now, the radio contact, the words of the distant correspondent and the images of the island, filled the couple's thoughts. Yet the contact also made the radio ham feel ill at ease since he still didn't know anything about this man he had been talking to for months, and by now he no longer dared ask him questions. And after hearing those words, he didn't feel like asking him to explain, thinking that the other would, as usual, not reply.

It was around this time that he he was given a device which enabled him to track his radio contacts. This is how he managed to locate the island off the coast of Scotland. At least he now knew where the house was, but what was going to happen to this man Archie?

If, for some reason, his eyes would soon no longer be able to look across the island, then his desire to talk about it while he could still see it was understandable. However, the young radio ham, unable to ask any questions, felt increasingly ill at ease with Archie. With the result that during their last few contacts he didn't even listen. He turned on the tape-recorder and left him to talk alone.

That is why he only noticed a month later — a month in which he neither received messages from his correspondent nor made contact himself — that on the last tape Archie had sent his greetings, thanked him for listening and said he would be leaving the island the next day.

Eight months passed. The couple left school and set off on a journey. They reached Glasgow and from there the little town of Oban on the west coast of Scotland. From Oban a boat took them to Archie's island.

When they disembarked, they immediately found the long road that went around the heather-covered headland. They recognized almost everything and could find their way about as if they had been there before. They recognized the point where the coastline was being eaten away by the sea and the igneous rocks disappeared at high tide. The ground above this point rose to form a small grassy promontory, which is where they expected Archie's house to come into view.

And there, in fact, was a cottage and behind the cottage an old grey house with a very low doorway. In the cottage there lived a fair-haired man with his fair-haired wife. Being unsure as to how to broach the subject of Archie, the couple asked whether there were any houses to rent, and the fair-haired man offered them the old grey stone house which he had just finished making habitable.

So the couple installed themselves in the house, and, wandering around the island day after day, they found the places

Archie had described. They found the city of wild rabbits — a dune full of tunnels that seemed like an underground metropolis. They found the paved path along the heather-covered headland where Archie had once seen the bones and fleece of a sheep that had been attacked by a hawk and where on other occasions he had seen the wild goats, almost five foot tall, that live on the headland. They found the immense raised beach on the east coast, half of which had fallen into the sea the previous year.

In the evenings they went and watched television in the cottage of the fair-haired couple. She was called Susan and he was called Archie.

They talked and talked with Susan and Archie, and then finally got round to broaching the subject that was on their minds. And so, when the owner of the house learned that the young man was none other than the distant radio contact, he told him Archie's story.

Archie was a policeman in Glasgow who had shot at a boy one night, and hit him in the heart. It was an accident, but Archie blamed himself for his utter negligence — the result of insensitivity to his surroundings and contempt for what he saw in those disreputable areas on the outskirts of Glasgow.

That night he was caught at the scene of the crime by another policeman, a friend of his. Archie admitted his guilt, but he also told his friend that he wasn't ready to face prison. He had asked him to let him and his wife go and live somewhere for five years, after which time he would return and give himself up. His friend had consented.

So the man had come to live on the island. Five years had passed during which time he had learnt to observe the things around him so as to teach himself to be more careful in his thoughts and actions, and had then returned to Glasgow to turn himself in.

By now the couple were confused. Who was Archie? And who was their landlord who knew the whole story and was himself called Archie?

Only a few evenings later did their landlord explain that he was the other policeman, the one who had allowed Archie to go away for five years. After that incident and after Archie's arrest, he no longer wanted to go on being a policeman, and had retired and come to live in Archie's cottage. By coincidence, he too was called Archie.

The following winter the couple from Gallarate got a letter. Their former landlord told them that the case against Archie had been dropped and that he was about to return to the island. His superiors had prevented him from pleading guilty, and the killing was simply regarded as a hazard of the job, like so many other murders of little consequence in those areas of Glasgow.

Now the two friends, Archie and Archie, were going to start raising sheep. If the couple ever happened to be in that part of the world, they would always be welcome.

A Japanese girl

I am going to tell the story of a Japanese girl I met in Los Angeles. She was small and slight, and used to live to the north of the city, right on the edge of the desert. To get to her house, you had to leave the city freeway, cross enormous bridges packed with trucks and cars in all eight lanes, exit to the north and out into a canyon, keep going as far as an Arco Station, and then turn right up a hill.

On arriving in the United States at the age of fifteen, she had got married almost immediately to some man from New York, and learnt to be a seamstress. Before long, she left the man and started consulting a 'reader of signs' or astrological adviser to find out what she should do in life.

The astrological adviser suggested that, given the position of certain stars, the east was not suitable for her, and it would be better for her to live in the west. So, the girl moved from New York to Los Angeles, where she found a downtown apartment and became a fashion designer.

She went on consulting her New York astrological adviser every week by phone, and one day he told her that it would be more suitable for her to live in a hilly area. So the girl moved to the extreme northern outskirts of the city, to an area that was in the hills and not far from the desert.

She used to spend the morning and early afternoon making up garments in her apartment with a student, a young Filipino girl who lived on the floor below. The apartment consisted of one long room without any partition, which had a rail full of clothes running across it at one end, lots of mannequins, thread and material everywhere, two folding-beds with oriental covers, a dressing-table, a formica-topped table and four chairs, a fridge and a gas cooker. A TV set that was never turned off stood on top of a small imitation marble pillar.

Every afternoon at 5.30 she used to sit at the dressing- table and start making herself up in front of the mirror, which had a bamboo frame, all the while smoking marijuana to help her relax. She usually made herself up in the traditional Japanese way — face all white and lips and eye-brows finely pencilled. Putting on this make-up took an hour-and-a-half, and sometimes the pencilling wasn't right so she had to start all over again. Her clothes, on the other hand, were in a European style of earlier times, and included a hat with a veil.

Every evening, she used to go to a recording studio and watch some famous singer's recording sessions from behind a glass panel. During the day, she would make one phone call after another in order to get hold of passes and gain admission to the recording studios. When she telephoned, she called herself by the French name she had assumed on becoming a fashion designer.

On the wall she kept a calendar on which she noted down the various recording sessions for which she had managed to get a pass. Almost every evening in the month was booked a month in advance. She used to fill in the spaces on the calendar with the names of the singers.

After the recording sessions, she went to dinner with the managers of the various record companies, fashion designers and advertising people who had obtained the passes for her. One evening, I saw her in a restaurant and heard her talking about work in her immigrant English, while the others nodded with approval, as if at an exercise well done.

On Thursday evenings, some of these fashion-designers and advertising people went skating somewhere in Cahuenga, I think, and the Japanese girl would also go skating on Thursdays in this remote spot, where she once saw the actress Shelley Duval.

At night from her windows it was possible to see the headlights of the cars going along the freeway at the foot of the hills, while beyond that lay an endless city, few of whose streets were known to the girl, or to myself or anyone else.

Through her work she got to know some Italians in Los Angeles — two women, one of them a fashion journalist and the other a fashion designer, and also a young shirt manufacturer — all of whom lived in an annexe of the Marmont Hotel on Sunset Boulevard. And, one Sunday morning, on her way to visit her new Italian friends, the girl saw the film star Anthony Perkins sunbathing on the hotel lawn.

At the Marmont Hotel, the young shirt manufacturer tried to woo her. However, for whole evenings at a time, the Japanese girl seemed not to notice that he had said anything at all, and she spoke only to the Italian fashion designer and the journalist.

The three women often discussed the famous stars they had seen about town, though they never remembered the names of the movies they had appeared in. On these occasions, the young Italian shirt manufacturer, who remembered the names of all the movies, their directors and even their dates, would break into the conversation. Yet the Japanese girl seemed not to hear him, and the other two women weren't particularly interested in such things.

So, at first he lost heart because the Japanese girl never looked at him, but then he resigned himself to the situation, and no longer even tried to take part in their conversations.

The following summer, the girl came to Milan and brought some of her designs with her. A major dealer in the fashion industry liked the designs very much and commissioned a series of twenty outfits, which were to be made up in Italy.

The girl rang her New York astrological adviser, who suggested finding an apartment that was at least ten miles from the city. After a lot of looking, and helped by the Italian fashion designer she had met in Los Angeles, she finally found an apartment in

Bollate in a large new block stuck in the countryside, exactly ten miles from the western-most outskirts of the city.

Some time later, the Italian fashion designer held a party at her house in Milan and invited the Japanese girl and the young shirt manufacturer. At the party the girl smoked marijuana and drank the whole evening, so by the end she had to be escorted to her car.

The young shirt manufacturer, who was trying to woo her once more, offered to accompany her.

He stood giving signals so that she could back out of via Bigli into via Manzoni and drive away.

She drove off, running into him as if she had not even noticed him there. When the fashion designer went to visit him in hospital, the young shirt manufacturer who had been hurt in the accident said that it had all been his fault. He had been aware for some time that it was a strain for the Japanese girl to notice him, to see him, and when she did see him, she always had to make a special effort to recognize him.

He also mentioned predestination, saying that we all follow a preordained path, that we all do what we can, and that to force destiny in a particular direction can be dangerous.

Every morning in Bollate, when the Japanese girl went to do the shopping, she had to pass in front of a very long concrete fortress in the middle of the fields which looked like a big prison because of its strange towers with turrets that face outwards as they do on prisons. This was an immigrant district — mainly Sicilian — and the unemployed men in the area used to go and hang around in front of a bar a few hundred yards from the fortress, staying there all day doing nothing. When the Japanese girl went by, the eyes of all the unemployed men followed her until she had disappeared around the corner.

I learnt subsequently that the place suited her and she never really noticed either the fortress that looked like a prison or the eyes of the unemployed men that followed her when she left the house. Her designs were a success and everything went as foreseen by the New York astrological adviser.

The young shirt manufacturer would have liked to marry her, but predestination did not allow for it.

The commuter children who got lost

They used to get on the train at Codogno every Friday, and the boy would go to Milan because his parents were separated; he had to spend five days with his father in Codogno and the weekend in Milan with his mother. The girl would go to Milan, since she was seeing a psychoanalyst on the advice of some doctor or other, which had met with the full approval of her father.

She was about thirteen, and he was about eleven. Since they both got bored at home always listening to their parents talking, they formed the idea that all parents are boring. Then they explored the idea, coming to the conclusion that all adults are boring. Finally, some things happened that made them think that all parents and adults are not only boring but idiotic — so idiotic, in fact, that it isn't worth taking any notice of what they say or do.

It happened like this. During their weekends in Milan, the two children went around seeing whether they could pick out someone in the street who wasn't boring. For example, they followed someone on a bus or in the underground, making bets saying: 'I bet that person's not boring.' And they kept a written record of the bets in a notebook.

However, after a while they got extremely bored, especially watching the people in the underground who don't know what to do with themselves as they're always frightened that others might be looking at them, or the people who want to show others they don't give a toss, or the people who want to show others they're fed up with everything. These things made them melancholy.

Then, they were made melancholy by drivers who blow their horn to show they're in a hurry, by people in the street who shove past to show they're just out for themselves, by people in bars who go on about things of no interest to anyone simply to show they can talk, people who laugh when there's nothing to laugh at just to show they know it all, people in shops who look from side to side to show they can't afford to waste time, and women who look to one side to show that they're there to be admired, etc., etc., etc.

Actually, everything they saw as they wandered around brought on a feeling of melancholy, and it was the same kind of melancholy that came over them when they were at home and heard their parents and relations talking.

They filled up the notebook with bets that neither of them ever won, because all the adults they came across were boring.

They followed a nice-looking old man right to the end of viale Corsica. All of a sudden, the old man collapsed on the ground and they ran to help him up, but the old man didn't listen and was only concerned about his coat; 'I must have got the back of my coat dirty,' he kept saying. Since his mind was entirely on his coat, and he didn't pay any attention to the children asking him how he was and whether he could walk, they left him to it. After taking a few steps, the old man fell to the ground again, and some passers-by said he had died of a heart attack. That old man was boring too.

On another occasion, they followed a woman dressed entirely in black and wearing dark glasses up corso Magenta, because the boy thought she might be nice. However, when she reached a parking space and gave an attendant some money saying, 'Here,' they realized from how she said that one word that she was a really boring woman — so much so that just thinking about it left the boy with a bad taste in his mouth.

On yet another occasion, they saw a man who looked drunk and followed him in the underground as far as a district I won't give the name of. Here, the man went to sit on a step next to some others who seemed equally drunk, and they all stayed there with their heads lolling backwards and forwards. At that moment, some shots rang out, and then someone pointed to a car speeding off. The children also ran off as fast as they could, afraid there might be further shooting.

While they were running, a car drew up and a man said: 'Quick, jump in.' In the car, they explained what had happened. The man told them it was a regular occurrence in that area: when the mafia people had to try out their weapons, they would drive by and shoot at the drug addicts sitting on the steps.

The man seemed nice and asked them to dinner at his house. He lived in a remote but beautiful place west of Malpensa airport, in a spot where there is an electricity plant with woods all around and a few isolated houses.

The children thought he was a teacher because of the books that took up almost the entire drawing-room. During dinner he spoke for two hours about things they didn't understand, and he appeared to them to be more intelligent than the average person. They fell asleep while the man was still talking.

An hour later, they were running away through the woods in the darkness, because when they were asleep the man started touching the girl's legs, and then, when they threw books at him, he pretended to laugh and said: 'It was only a joke.'

The two children told me they had got away that time largely because this particular adult seemed such a cretin, and just thinking about him left a bad taste in their mouths.

By this time, the children had already changed as a result of their experiences. They no longer played the game with the bets written down in the notebook, but still used to spend the weekends going around Milan.

One Sunday in December, wandering around in the midst of a fog in a part of the city with large new blocks of flats — out towards Monza, I think — they came across a woman who was lost. She was middle-aged, wearing a tracksuit and had a woolly hat on her head. That morning, she had gone out jogging and couldn't find her way home. She questioned everbody she met, telling them she lived in a large block of flats like those that could be seen in the distance — blocks that were identical to one another throughout the area.

The children, who landed up there by chance, heard her repeatedly telling everyone the name of her road, each time adding: 'G Block, Staircase 38.' A small crowd gathered around her, and some children pointed to a row of white blocks of flats as if they knew where G Block was. The woman immediately set off in that direction, followed by a procession of children, gentlemen with dogs, and people in tracksuits.

The two children also joined the procession of helpers.

On arriving in the forecourt of a huge block, which was in fact G Block, the helpers saw that the name on the bell in Staircase 38 did not correspond to that of the woman. So everyone started to drift off, because their search had come to an end and it was lunchtime.

The two children found themselves alone with the lost woman and, following her, they left the forecourt. They crossed a field full of fog, and from then on the further they went the thicker the fog became; they were in another area with huge blocks of flats, and by now they too had lost their way.

They crossed wide avenues where there was no one to be seen, then found themselves in open country, and then back in areas like the ones they had been in earlier where the woman was wandering aimlessly around. Every now and again the woman asked them to read the road signs or tell her the names of the places they were going through, and the children replied: 'We're not from Milan.'

Then on leaving another built-up area, they couldn't see anything anymore. They must have been in open country — they were crossing frozen fields and it was white all around. They had never seen fog so white, nor a fog so thick that they had to test the ground in front of them with their feet before taking a step, because they could scarcely see beyond the end of their noses.

They had to stop. As they turned around in the fog, they saw a great white wall surrounding them on all sides and could no longer locate each other, nor see their own bodies, nor clearly make out each other's voices. They were cold and lonely, but could go neither forwards nor backwards, and had to stay where they were in that strangest of places where they had got lost.

They had come a long way in their search for something that wasn't boring without ever finding anything, and now who knows how long they would have to stay in the fog, cold and melancholy, before being able to go home to their parents. That is when they came to suspect that all life might be like this.

What happened to the three footballing brothers

This is the story of three brothers who showed what exceptional footballers they were during a tournament for junior teams. They were the talk of the outskirts where they lived, and even supporters of other teams would go and watch them play every Sunday morning on pitches on the edges of Milan.

One was seventeen, the other two were twins aged fifteen, and all three of them were forwards. Apart from their shooting ability and ball-control, which already seemed up to professional standards, the three always knew how to find one another with skilful passes, as if each of them always knew where the others would be running to without needing to look.

The manager of the team was a greengrocer who was rich thanks to having a stall at the market of a nearby town, and he was always a slightly mysterious figure because of the mirrored sun glasses he wore when he was watching matches involving his players. He was very satisfied with the three, and called them his 'little champions'.

The three brothers won many matches for the team, and on one occasion they played an away game at the big San Siro stadium in Milan before an evening match between two famous international teams.

At San Siro the trainers of the two big city clubs saw the three play and were astounded. After the match, some men in black went to talk to them, asking whether they felt up to coming to Milan to train with the apprentices of a big club.

When the greengrocer heard that his players had been approached by these men in black, he flew into a rage. In fact, he was in the process of organizing an apprentices' team at that very moment, following an agreement with two well-established clubs, and he didn't want anyone setting eyes on his three brothers. Indeed, he did his best to see that sports writers mentioned their talent as little as possible.

To settle the matter, he went to discuss it with the parents of the three, and convinced them to sign a contract which stipulated that the brothers were to become his property, as players, for a two-year period.

The training sessions for the first boys selected by the greengrocer as apprentices began.

In the first league match the three brothers didn't play well because they didn't feel at ease with their team mates, and their team lost.

They also played badly in the next match and, in the third one, while they were in the changing-rooms waiting to go onto the field, they began to wet themselves. They were sitting on a bench, watching the diarrhoea as it trickled down their legs. So, they didn't play, and the trainer told them this often happened before an important match because young players got too worked up.

The following Sunday, they were playing another away game at the San Siro stadium in Milan. There was a punch-up in mid-field involving two players, who got sent off, and straight afterwards one of the twins wet himself and simply couldn't move. He had to go off, his team was left with nine players on the field and lost the match.

That evening, the greengrocer manager slapped the three brothers across the face, cursing heavily. The next day, he went to discuss the situation with their parents.

Since the three were still over-anxious, the manager proposed that they be sent to a summer retreat along with the other boys in the apprentices' team who weren't performing as they should be. 'They're still too young. They need to grow up,' he said.

The summer retreat, in an isolated house right in the middle of a deserted valley, was secret. All the boys and the boys' parents promised not to talk about it to anyone.

It was run by an old gym-teacher who began by making his pupils run all day long, wearing them out and irritating them into the bargain by insisting they run back and forth through bramble bushes.

Moreover, he tested out their nerves in other ways. He used to give them half-an-hour off in the courtyard of the house, all the while studying the childish gestures they made. Then, he lined them up and ordered one of them to repeat a particular gesture, which inevitably looked childish. Then, the teacher explained to everyone that it was just the kind of gesture 'queers' use.

So, the pupils no longer knew what gestures to use and always kept their hands in their pockets to avoid giving themselves away. Moreover, the boy shown up by the teacher got called 'queer' for the rest of the day by his companions. And it ended up that by evening the pupils, tired from all their running and irritated by the bramble scratches, beat the hell out of one another in the dormitory.

The old teacher intervened on such occasions with a whip in his hand. He made whoever was responsible for the fight come forward — usually the 'queer' as it happened — asking him whether he still wanted to go through with the apprenticeship and become a real pro. When he said 'yes', he ordered him to pull down his pants, bend over a stool, and let himself be beaten by all his companions without complaining, to show he was a man.

Some didn't manage to hide their pain, and for them the next day began with the same torture. On the other hand, anyone who didn't protest at the pain proved himself a man in the eyes of the teacher and his companions.

Consequently, after a week, the number of participants at the retreat had fallen by half. Many of them had not been able to endure the torture and had given up trying to become real pros.

The following weeks were devoted to other exercises, all designed to make the pupils less nervous, by straining their nerves as much as possible. 'You must grow up,' said the teacher, 'and you must stop behaving like women.'

During the last fortnight, the boys were left locked up inside the house. Their clothes were confiscated; beds, chairs, and all supplies of food taken away. The pupils slept naked on the ground, and, naturally, after a couple of days, they were as hungry as wolves.

Every two days or so, the teacher appeared without warning. He placed plates of food on the ground at the far end of a long corridor which ran down three sides of the house and led to the dormitory where the boys slept.

This corridor was rather narrow. Therefore, when without warning the teacher gave the signal, the pupils hurled themselves out of the dormitory and, wild with hunger, had to viciously kick and shove one another since the first to reach the plates gulped down all the food, and the others went without for days on end.

However, there was more to being successful than just viciously kicking and shoving the others aside. 'If you want to get on in life, never let yourself be caught off guard,' warned the old teacher.

To begin with, the pupils had to spend all their time in the dormitory, and could only dive out of the room when the siren was sounded by the teacher. At least one in three calls was a false alarm, and so the pupils, by the time they had fought their way to the end of the corridor, often found nothing to eat.

Then, the pupils had to be ready to race out of the dormitory at the slightest sound for the teacher would set off the siren without warning. Yet, to do this, they had to spend the remainder of the day resting naked and famished on the ground so as to be in peak condition when it came to leaping up and shoving the others aside.

'Finally,' the teacher explained, 'you must learn to stay calm in order to take advantage of the fact that others suffer from nerves and lose their heads.'

People who have experienced this type of apprenticeship maintain that the methods described here have beneficial effects which last for the rest of a player's career. However, for the three brothers this wasn't to be the case.

At the first important match, all three played extremely badly. They were confused by everything going on around them — confused by the referee's whistle, by the ball which rolled slowly out of play as if it were dying, by the desolate look on an opponent's face, or even by a kleenex on the ground. By now in a state of unrelieved tension, they tried to pay attention to everything, so the slightest thing confused them.

During the next match, one of the twins fainted on the field, and their team suffered a resounding defeat. Afterwards, in the changing-rooms, the boys were all so nervous that they threw their boots at one another's heads, and they were blindly hitting one another when their manager came in.

The greengrocer manager slapped each of them across the face in turn, and then said: 'Next time, if you're nervous, kick the shit out of the others, don't fight among yourselves.'

The three brothers pleaded over and again with their parents not to make them play, contract or no contract, saying: 'We're not good enough.' However, their mother and father used to reply that they were throwing away a golden opportunity out of sheer wilfulness; indeed, everyone thought they were up-and-coming players, and would in a few years be ready to play in the First Division.

One night, the three of them stole a large lorry with a trailer and fled in the direction of Switzerland. However, on the way, they ended up in a ditch, smashing up the trailer.

Caught by the police after a long overnight chase near the border, they were sent to a reformatory. And here the three went back to playing football — once again the exceptional players they used to be.

Now they're in a reformatory in the province of Mantua. They keep on getting into trouble in order to stay in the reformatory as long as possible, scared stiff at the prospect of some day having to go back into the outside world.

The story of an apprenticeship

When he was in Los Angeles, the narrator of this story lived for a long time in the villa of a Greek film producer who used to produce third-rate films for export to Arab countries or to the Far East. He had stopped writing stories because he had never got anywhere in this line of work. He had decided never to go back to Europe again, and was counting on being asked to take up a teaching post at some university in this part of the world.

He used to spend much of the day looking at old American films on TV in a big room on the second floor of the villa — a room full of exotic plants, ample leather armchairs, small fish-tanks and African sculptures, some of which reached up to the ceiling. Every afternoon at five o'clock, he used to have to go out for a walk because it was around that time that he felt like crying. He would go for a stroll along Wilshire, and spent hours admiring the shop windows.

The producer who was putting him up used to work by the side of his pool, holding the screenplay of some box-office success in one hand and dictating to a director the changes needed in order to produce an almost identical but third-rate version of the film. The director took notes and these were then passed on to a couple of screenwriters who used to work, together with a typist, in a small house next to the villa.

The two screenwriters, husband and wife, always used to dress identically, in identical dark suits and identical silk shirts, and came to work in two identical black cars. They used to work separately, dividing up the scenes to be written, and they never spoke to each other. They never spoke to each other because that's the advice they had been given by a healer of souls whom they had been seeing for many years.

So, apart from exchanging essential information during the course of the day, the screenwriting couple only communicated with each other three evenings a week, with the healer of souls as mediator.

Whenever the screenwriting couple saw the narrator of this story wandering around the villa, they would give him suspicious looks as they thought he was a well-known European screen-writer come to replace them. And besides, the producer didn't hide the fact that he was unhappy with their work and intended to replace them for the next film. What's more, he didn't like either of them.

This is why one day, when he stopped to have a word with the husband under a palm tree that overhung the small house next-door to the villa, the man sparked off a crisis.

The wife immediately wanted to know from the husband what he'd been talking about with that man under the palm tree. However, the husband, following the instructions of the healer of souls, did not reply. So, the wife suspected that the two men had come to an agreement to write the next filmscript together, and leave her out.

At the height of the row, when the husband at last decided to speak and admitted to wanting to be rid of the wife, she attacked him with a pair of scissors and seriously hurt one of his fingers.

It was getting on for mid September. Upset by the incident, the man suddenly decided to leave Los Angeles. At six o'clock one morning, he called a taxi and left the villa without saying anything to anyone.

One rainy day he broke his journey at an airport in Nevada, and during the stop-over he went to a lavatory to cry. He arrived in Wichita one night, aboard a small plane with no more than fifteen passengers, and from there continued his journey by bus in the direction of the small town of Alden, Kansas.

His new house had a small gate in front, and on the other side of this wooden gate there was a lawn that ran down to the road. The town had eight tarmac roads and two hundred and twenty inhabitants whose average age was sixty.

All around the town were fields planted with wheat — pieces of land of equal size that had been granted to settlers a century earlier and still belonged to the same families. Outside the town there were just dirt-roads, and every afternoon the man used to walk as far as a river that flows through that part of the country.

He was the guest of a white-haired old couple whom he had got to know in Europe some years earlier.

The couple who were putting him up had gone on a trip to Europe some years earlier, and the man had accompanied them on visits to various Italian cities. During the trip the wife, Edith, had kept a diary. Then, on their return, she had spent her evenings for about two years giving readings from this travel diary to almost every one of the two hundred and twenty inhabitants of the village.

These evening readings were a great success, and many passages were read again in public, either in a large room which had been converted into a restaurant, or in the room of a hotel about ten miles away.

So, when in the course of a fortnight the man was introduced to each of the two hundred and twenty inhabitants of Alden, they all said how very happy they were to know, in person, a character from the celebrated diary.

The mayor of the town, a tiny woman in her seventies, told him she had pictured him as smaller and with a moustache. The young cashier from the local bank asked him, since he was a European personality, to say something to her in French, which the man did, eliciting an enthusiastic response from the entire population. So much so, that the following evening in the local restaurant he had to repeat the very words that he had spoken in French in the the bank. And the man who ran the newly converted restaurant, an ex-music teacher, played the French song 'La vie en rose' on the violin in his honour.

Each time Bill, the husband, introduced the man to someone as they went from one house to another, he used to repeat exactly the same joke. And on each occasion the wife, Edith, used to laugh as if hearing it for the first time. When there was a repeat public reading of parts of the diary in a hotel ten miles away, Bill still made the same joke when he introduced the man. And the entire audience, who had already heard it before, burst out laughing as if hearing it for the first time. So the man then began to laugh too as if hearing it for the first time, as that seemed the right thing to do.

Later, he was asked to give a short talk to the children of the junior school in a nearby town, and he agreed to do so. He then agreed to repeat the same talk in two other schools, adding, as requested, a few words in French on each occasion for the benefit of the adults present. By doing exactly what was asked of him he felt more at peace, and during the day he no longer felt like crying.

Every evening he used to go and visit a family, or go to a public meeting, and on Sunday mornings he went to the service in the Methodist chapel. When he went to chapel, he wanted to show that he understood the importance of appearances, and so he was clean-shaven, he dressed his best, put some of Bill's brilliantine on his hair, and even plucked the hairs out from his ears.

After about a month he started to get numerous letters and cards from relatives of the inhabitants of Alden, who congratulated him on his reputation in that village where all spoke well of him. The son of the owners of the post office sent him his best wishes and invited him to come to Ottawa whenever he wanted. Two of the mayor's daughters invited him to stay in Hudson, in New York State. Bill and Edith's son sent him a little Chinese cage with a delightful papier mâché bird inside.

The man wrote letters of thanks to each of them, trying to imitate the words and tone Bill and Edith used in carrying out the ceremonial tasks that marked each moment of their lives.

Around Christmas time, he went to visit the mayor's daughters in Hudson, to the north of New York. He stayed near a beech wood and almost stopped crying altogether, except sometimes on waking. When he was introduced to their neighbours and acquaintances as a celebrity, he always felt a moment's panic, but for the most part he managed to do what was required of him.

He had to catch a plane back to Europe on Christmas Day. The afternoon of Christmas Eve he spent wandering around the streets of New York which were filled with people, cheerful and laden with presents, pouring out of the shops and onto the pavement in peaceful, orderly and cheerful crowds.

That evening he went to dinner in Queens, with an Italian family.

On that occasion many guests were seated around a long table all talking at once and making endless toasts, and overhead festoons of coloured lights flashed on and off. The man, once he had told the story of his journey to Kansas, realized that everyone here was also treating him as a celebrity who has duly presented his credentials.

And throughout that evening's send-off he was to be treated as a person of consequence — so much so that in order to return the compliment and make people laugh, he had repeated some of Bill's jokes. By this time he was a man of some maturity, and a man who, that day, had combed his hair, shaved, put on a nice red tie, and come to a realization of what life is: a web of ceremonial relationships which hold together something that has no substance.

Some months later, in Piacenza, he finally accepted his situation, and he no longer felt like crying. He had also accepted that he could not be the celebrity that he had been in Kansas, though the rituals he had learnt there were not to be forgotten. So, now that it was all so distant, he was even able to write the story of his apprenticeship with Bill and Edith — in other words, this one.

A barber's life after death

There was a barber who had come to Piacenza to do his military service at a time when the city was full of barracks and, consequently, full of soldiers on the streets. And this is going back to the war when the barber got to know a girl from Piacenza and married her. Taken prisoner by the Germans and sent to work in Germany, only some years later did the barber return to his wife's part of the world, where he opened a barber's shop. His wife opened a hair-dressing business above that barber's shop in the country.

Time went by, and one evening on his way home, the barber thought he saw on the outside landing a friend who wasn't there; in fact, he had died a good many years earlier in Albania. He confided what had happened to his wife and she suggested that he go to hospital for treatment, since she didn't feel like being with someone who had hallucinations. The barber accepted what she said and was admitted to an asylum.

He remained in the asylum for about a year, and then for a further two years, before he was finally discharged and sent back home.

In the meantime, his wife had both moved house and transferred the business to the city, where she opened a hair-dresser's. And it was here, one fine day, that the barber showed up.

His wife told him she didn't feel up to having him in the house as he had only just left the asylum; the whole thing was too recent and she wanted to be sure that her husband really had fully recovered and wouldn't have any more hallucinations. The barber accepted this and went back to living in the house in the country, above the old shop.

In the months that followed, the man showed no sign of imbalance and never mentioned anything about hallucinations to anyone. From time to time, he took his bicycle and went to the city to see his wife, asking her on each occasion whether she was ready to have him back.

The wife showed she had less and less time to spare on him, being so taken up with her hair-dressing. In the end, she asked him once and for all not to visit her ever again.

The barber accepted this, but afterwards began to think that his wife was denying him his existence. And he laid the matter before his customers who came to have their hair cut in his old barber's shop in the country, saying his wife was denying him his existence and this was something he could not accept.

He began to think that everyone else was denying him his existence too, just like his wife; in other words, in the street, in the bar, in offices, people showed that they didn't think of him as being alive. He maintained that this was due to an event that had taken place during the war, when, one night, on the banks of the river Trebbia, a German soldier had shot at him and missed. Evidently, everyone thought that the German soldier had hit and killed him, and that therefore he had not been alive for a good while.

After convincing himself of this, he began to go every Sunday and search the pebbly bed of the Trebbia with a fishing net. He searched along the river bed under the bank where the German soldier had shot at him that night, looking for the bullet, which having missed him, must have finished up on the river bed.

He spoke to his customers about some thing, lost among the pebbles of the Trebbia, on which his life depended. Though, he never used the word 'life', and spoke always of his 'sistence'.

Seeing him in the water every Sunday inspecting the river bed, the fishermen on the Trebbia would sometimes, for a laugh, ask him if he was looking for proof of God's existence. Each time he replied: 'No, I'm looking for proof that I exist.'

Some months after the death of the barber, his wife discovered that she was pregnant, and she spread the rumour that she was expecting the dead barber's child. Later on, she also spread the rumour that the barber had spoken to her at night, saying that he was delighted that she recognized the child as his, for this meant she had stopped denying him his existence.

According to the woman, the barber had continued to speak to her at night on many further occasions, always maintaining that his sistence had not yet come to an end. Until the day she married again and moved to another city, and from that time on the barber spoke no more.

On the value of appearances

There is a woman, no longer as young as she was, who has for a great many years been a cleaning lady in various middle-class homes in Cremona. The story goes that, scarcely out of an orphanage, she met a man known as the 'Calabrian', who got her pregnant and married her, only to disappear from the scene soon afterwards — first because he was wanted for a robbery and then because he was in prison for the said robbery.

From then on, the woman worked as a cleaning lady, and it is said that she set aside a lot of money, saving every lira she earned at work all those years, by eating only her employers' leftovers, or the leftovers she collected in restaurants late at night. With her savings she would buy a flat, which she would give to her son when he decided to get married.

The woman's son, a fat and lazy-looking man of about twenty-five, was in and out of prison for petty theft and dealing in stolen goods. He left prison not so long ago, and lived with his mother, and was supported by her. However, in prison he learnt to paint, it seems, and subsequently devoted himself to this activity, painting nude portraits of famous actresses which he managed to sell without much difficulty.

As for the man known as the 'Calabrian', he reappeared some time ago on the outskirts of Cremona, and did well enough for a while, thanks perhaps to a series of arson attacks on warehouses — a remunerative line of work this, in which he was apparently an expert. However in subsequent years he didn't do at all well; dishevelled and maybe ill, he lived in the basement of an abandoned factory together with his young girlfriend and worked on and off at a scrap car dealer's. Motivated by a desire to renew contact with his son, or so he said, he regularly turned up at the house of the wife he had deserted, always whining for money and invariably getting thrown out and sworn at.

Recently, a solicitor to whom the woman had turned for advice over investing a sum of money, received a visit from the 'Calabrian' who wanted to find out about his wife's estate. He explained that he was sick and needed treatment, and that as she was still his wife, she had a duty to help him.

Summoned by the solicitor a week later, the 'Calabrian' and his wife had a violent argument which ended up in the street. Here, the woman took from her bag a stone she had deliberately brought with her, and threw it at the head of her so-called husband.

The man was taken to hospital and the woman was accused of malicious wounding. However, at this point something cropped up which changed the course of events.

Shortly afterwards, the 'Calabrian' was again summoned to the solicitor's office. His wife, through the solicitor, asked him to attend his son's wedding. The son, in fact, had got to know a young and lovely girl and was about to get married, and it was only right that the husband should be present.

The 'Calabrian' refused to attend his son's wedding, on the grounds, he said, that he didn't have any decent clothes to wear and thus would only make a bad impression. At which the woman agreed to clothe him from head to foot, provided he came.

However, the 'Calabrian' refused a second time because, he said, he couldn't come to the wedding without his young girlfriend and without a decent present for the bride and groom — a present he didn't have the means to buy. At this, the woman withdrew her previous offer. She said she didn't want the girlfriend even mentioned, and that the wedding would go ahead without him. Unless, that is, in return for the money to buy a washing-machine as a present, he undertake to come to the wedding alone.

The 'Calabrian' explained that he would be very happy to accept, but that he didn't feel like going to the wedding on foot, because everyone had always known him as a car lover. What would he like? A small car. The woman undertook to give him the money for a small car the moment he withdrew the accusation of malicious wounding, and so this particular episode was brought to an end. The woman then went to a printer where she got a hundred or so invitations to the wedding reception printed — invitations to be sent to all the families in whose houses she had worked, to solicitors, doctors, rich tradesmen, restaurant owners, and teachers from the city, not to mention her other acquaintances.

That same morning she went into an electrical goods shop and bought a dish-washer and a TV set with a huge screen. She then bought, in the shop next door, a green parrot which kept on saying: 'Good evening, good morning.'

By the time she left the roadside café where she had negotiated the price of a wedding reception for at least a hundred guests, almost nothing remained of the money she had spent thirty-odd years saving. But now that she had fixed up her son — seeing him married and making him a present of the flat she had bought beforehand — she didn't need much to keep her going.

The roadside café where the wedding reception was held was a large room full of tables covered with paper serviettes. An open oven behind the counter showed that the place was little more than a pizzeria for motorists travelling along the Lower Po road.

On the day of the wedding, as the guests were arriving, it became clear that far too many tables had been laid.

There arrived the groom, fat and looking wrecked, and the young bride wearing a silk dress with a train. There then arrived six tenants from the building where the groom's mother lived, and a young man with a little goatee and a moustache whom nobody recognized. There was also the solicitor, who would later say something to the groom's mother and then leave early. There was a man with a crumpled jacket and trousers, who was the owner of the scrap car business where the groom's father worked from time to time.

And finally there was a rather well-known tennis player, whom the groom's mother had managed to persuade to come at the very last minute, in order to lend an air of importance to the wedding, given that no doctor, teacher or accountant had accepted the invitation.

As yet there was no sign either of the groom's father or of his present. The solicitor took the groom's mother to one side, and told her: 'Your husband is a swindler and I would be happy to bring a case against him.'

Then, in a corner, he said he felt it his duty, as her solicitor, to explain to her what he had found out only half an hour earlier.

He had discovered that the young bride was none other than the husband's girlfriend, whom the 'Calabrian' had introduced to his son so that he could marry and take possession of the flat. Furthermore, the self-same 'Calabrian' had already installed himself in the flat she had bought with her savings and made over to her son only a few days before. Lastly, the three of them intended to cohabit, and the crying shame was that no legal action could prevent this outrage.

At first, the woman was shattered by the revelation that she had been swindled. Then, she turned to look across the room and saw that no one had noticed the absence of her husband — as though he didn't exist — since they were all listening to the famous tennis player recounting what had happened to him at a tournament he had played in in Australia.

The woman thought it over for a minute, and said to the solicitor: 'Well, everthing's fine for now.' Then she explained: 'If nobody notices anything, it's as if nothing had happened.'

The solicitor replied that some day or other someone would notice that something had happened. So the woman dismissed him with the words: 'Yes, but until then I can pretend not to know anything and be happy that nothing has happened.'

Later, as many passing motorists had come in and recognized

the famous tennis player, she invited them to join the other guests, and she invited everyone who came in to sit down and eat. So, in the end, the large room was full of people and it would have been hard to imagine a better reception because everyone thought that everyone else was a proper guest and that the newly weds had lots of friends.

Only at the end of the meal, when even the wedding cake had been eaten, did the groom's father arrive. Well dressed, smiling, apologizing for his lateness, he drew everyone's attention to a large sports car parked in the road, which he had bought that morning at a knock-down price.

None of the guests took any notice because no one knew who he was, except for the scrap car dealer, who made the following comment: 'A car loses half its value the moment it's bought, and once something goes wrong it's time to get rid of it. Sooner or later they all end up at my yard, on the scrap heap — all on the scrap heap — because they're not built to last. So, what's the point of working yourself into the ground to earn money and spend it on cars? It's like throwing money down the drain.'

Time passing

A woman goes to work by car every day, travelling about fifty kilometres there and back. The hardest moment of her day is when, on the return journey, she finds herself back on the roads near her home, and starts to listen to the time passing.

On the other side of Cremona, going east along the Lower Po road, there is a big shopping centre whose sign can be seen from a long way off. Two long, low supermarkets with a twin car park alongside the slow lane take up an enormous space in the middle of the countryside. Piped music is played in the car parks, every now and again a voice announces a special offer, and there's the sound of the whistles of the security-men directing traffic in the parking area. Whole families who have come from the surrounding countryside get out of their cars to do their shopping. And as she passes by, the woman always notices how they all move a little uneasily, adrift in the open space along with thousands of others like them.

Immediately after that there is a village called Cicognolo, and from there on, leaving the Lower Po road behind, the lines of the landscape stretch out evenly all the way to the low horizon in the distance. Far off there can be seen straight roads punctuated at regular intervals by telegraph poles, and occasionally a lorry and sometimes a tractor driving along. Here, every evening, the woman is struck by the strange silence she always finds in the countryside.

Until, that is, she reaches those small houses with terraced gardens, and the rows of small two-storey houses, with balconies, outside staircases and flowers everywhere. At that point a distinct feeling suggests that the pervasive silence is not the silence found in open spaces; it is a residential silence that surrounds the villages and spreads into the countryside.

The woman says that round there you can see cars but no sign of dogs or children. As if their only purpose in life was to protect themselves from irritations, embarrassments, or complications, the owners live hidden in their little houses, emerging into the open solely in order to go to work or do the shopping in the supermarket.

No one can even remember any more what could possibly exist out there, apart from the hours that make up the day and the time that passes. So in the space filled by the residential silence there is only the time passing, and the time passing can be felt because the silence slows it down so much that it never seems to pass at all.

No one can hear the far off noises made by other people any more — noises that tell us that out there life goes on. And the people shut in their houses do little but wonder about the absence of noise as they wait for lunch-time, dinner-time, or the time to turn the television on. However, since time stretches like a piece of elastic the more people think about it, the occupants often find themselves inside their houses living in fear of the minute that never passes.

Going through a village by the name of Pieve San Giacomo, the woman often feels a sort of solidarity with its inhabitants, all of them shut in at home thinking. On the outskirts of the village there is a huge estate agent's sign, and she rarely sees a living soul in this village, barring the occasional heavily clad woman who cycles past and immediately disappears.

After the level-crossing, there is a road of small residential houses, just like a model, and that is where the woman lives. A more expensive house than the others has an enormous lawn and on the lawn a Molossian hound which never moves and wears the fixed expression of a statue; in other, less expensive, houses, garden gnomes from a Walt Disney film are placed beside the front door. Many of the façades of these small houses are covered with tiles, and in front of the houses there are miniature trees, minute lawns and beds of ostentatious flowers.

Often the woman doesn't feel like going back home to find her parents watching television in a kind of *rigor mortis* that goes with waiting for time to pass. So, she goes on as far as San Daniele Po and beyond, taking the B road to Casalmaggiore. And here too there are more long rows of small residential houses lining the road. Many of them are rustic-style dwellings like in a model and have walls covered in imitation stone and a path of crazy-paving running across the lawn as far as the gate. The lawn is often covered in daisies, and in front of the house there are fake wells made of plaster, miniature trees and ornamental laurel or magnolia bushes. In many of the gardens there are Hollywood-style swimming pools in miniature versions.

As she looks at these small houses, the woman is frequently struck by the endless minutiae that must have taken up the thoughts of their inhabitants. To the extent that, when looking at them, she gets the impression that the surrounding emptiness is something infinitely more ordered, more minutely organized than she could ever have imagined — like an intricate trap set to keep shame and uncertainty at bay, ridding life of anything of consequence.

She says that in this web of inconsequence, time is just time, that's all — timeless time in that it leads nowhere whatsoever. And the inhabitants, poor things, being caught in this trap, have become so confused that the *rigor mortis* that goes with waiting steals over them at the slightest upset.

Sometimes on her evening wanderings, she stops by at a bar in the square in San Daniele. There are always boys sitting in a row outside the bar, listening to the juke-box slumped in their chairs as if in a dream. She doesn't know why but as she looks at these boys, all her opinions and judgements about everything that she sees around her — about the small houses and their inhabitants — just seem utterly pointless. Not the slightest desire to judge anything anymore — let it all pass by, go wherever it has to go; after all, she says, it's only time passing.

What makes the world go on

In a small village in the province of Parma, not far from the Po, I was told the story of an old printer who had retired from work because he wanted finally to write a pamphlet he had been thinking about for ages. His pamphlet was to have dealt with the subject: what makes the world go on.

Being retired, the old printer spent the whole day going around on his moped, and as he went around, he used to read everything written that he came across. In fact, he had always liked reading and had always thought that, in order to understand what makes the world go on, it is necessary to read a lot.

With time, however, he noticed that he could not lift his eyes without finding some printed word to read.

Advertisements, sign boards, shop-window signs, walls covered with posters — all contributed to the fact that after half a day outside, he had already read thousands and thousands of printed words. So, on returning home, he no longer wanted to read books nor do any writing but just wanted to watch football matches on television.

He began to think he would never manage to write his pamphlet because there was too much to read. However, since starting to go around on his moped and see more and more printed words, more and more posters and advertisements everywhere, he decided that he at least wanted to know what had happened: why was the number of words to read everywhere always growing? Something must have happened.

He went to talk it over with the big meat wholesaler who imported meat from Russia and who, by making regular trips to Russia, might perhaps have found out what had happened. The wholesaler just said that people thought they were better off eating a lot of meat, so he had to get hold of all the meat they wanted, and this is why he had to go to Russia, where, as far as he knew, nothing had happened.

The printer went to the University of Parma. Here he found only students who didn't know anything about it, and lecturers who spent their life talking and all this talking had, in his opinion, driven them all quite mad. He realized that he couldn't get any help there either.

In the afternoons he often took his small niece around in the basket of the moped, and he used to explain his problem to her. His niece advised him to go and talk to her science teacher, who lived outside the village and was also a young inventor.

The young inventor had long hair down to his shoulders and always wore a mechanic's overall. He told the printer that he had never before given the problem any thought; so, the three of them — the printer, his small niece and the inventor — started to think about it.

Since, according to the printer, you always needed to start afresh with the problem of what makes the world go on, the three started from scratch. They thought about it and discussed it, and arrived at this initial conclusion: that the world goes on because people think about it; that is, they think about keeping it going.

But how do people think about it? What is thinking? At this point, the three of them (especially the child who was very enthusiastic about scientific studies) bought themselves scientific magazines at the newsagents, instalments of an encyclopedia and some books, and began studying. They learnt that external and internal impulses consist of an electric current that travels along the nerves as far as the axons or threads that pop out from the brain cells, passing via points called synapses where they (the impulses) have to make a small jump; apparently, a depolarization then takes place just as in car batteries, and the brain thus is nothing more than electrical circuitry in a state of constant flux.

I don't know much about their studies, except for the fact that the hopeless conclusions they reached were made public in the bar one day by the printer. In the bar he explained that no one is able to say — nor was there any magazine or encyclopedia that explains it — how anyone manages to remember a bowl of soup they've eaten a month earlier, given that there is no longer any electrical trace of that soup in the brain.

The three then devoted themselves to practical experiments using an encephalograph bought by the inventor at a liquidator's auction. They studied the different types of waves produced by the brain according to whether someone is asleep, awake, drowsy or angry. Then they moved on to do experiments with a pot plant.

They attached two electrodes connected to the encephalograph to the leaves of the plant, and watched the plant react in different ways when someone went and stood in front of it. The waves that could be read on the monitor of the encephalograph changed their pattern depending on what the person in front of the plant was doing or thinking. For example, one day the young inventor gave the girl a slap, and the pattern on the monitor became a mass of peaks as if the plant had taken offence. On another occasion, he said a number of flattering things in the ear of the school caretaker who had been positioned in front of the plant. And on the monitor there appeared gentle, as opposed to jagged, waves like the waves produced in the brain of someone asleep.

These findings encouraged the three to try and understand, with the aid of a plant and the encephalograph, what people are thinking. They began by asking themselves: what, for instance, do the rich think?

They borrowed a van and went and parked at night in front of the houses of the rich people in the area. While the girl and the printer kept a look-out on the road, the young inventor shinned over a garden wall and went and fixed the electrodes to the branches of a tree close to a window of one of the houses. Then, they recorded the types of waves that appeared on the monitor of the encephalograph in the van.

Such houses always have trees outside with branches that come right up to the windows. By fixing the electrodes to a suitable branch, the three hoped to find out, through the tree's reactions, what was going on in the heads of the people who were permanently shut up inside these houses watching television. Are they still alive, already dead, or only asleep? Do they or don't they think, or are they only dreaming that something is happening?

They carried on making these expeditions for most of the summer, accumulating a huge quantity of graphs. They compared one graph with another, compared their graphs with graphs reproduced in books, and in the end realized that they didn't understand anything that was happening.

Then, they got the idea of writing a letter to the mayor to lay before him all their failed projects. The mayor passed the letter on to the councillor responsible for Arts and Recreation, who organized a public conference on the question that the three felt so passionately about, that is: What Makes the World Go On?

A speaker was invited who went around addressing conferences on every conceivable topic, never failing to bring in his childhood and his memories. In less than an hour he resolved the problem, answered all the objections raised by the printer, the girl and the inventor, and brought the conference to an end. The public applauded, delighted to learn that there is a world out there that is so easy to explain that one can find a way of doing it in half an hour.

Then everyone, the minute they left the hall and were back in the street, immediately forgot what they had heard, the speaker forgot what he had said, and the following day no one could even remember anymore what the conference was about. In the small village everything goes on as before, except for the fact that there are more and more words on the walls, more and more signs, and more and more advertisements wherever the printer turns his eyes.

A parable for the disenchanted

There was a student from Parma who once read two novels by Knut Hamsun and immediately afterwards began writing short stories at night. He emigrated to France, to Montpellier, where he found work in a large garage with its own workshop.

He worked as a cashier in a glass box near the exit. From here he used to see the mechanics signalling to tell him, car by car, what type of repair they had carried out. When the customers passed the glass box, he had to total the cost of the labour and the price of the spare parts and add on a percentage for tax.

During lunch breaks, he used to eat at the university canteen, a big glass and concrete building with long tables and wooden benches. Here he made many friends. It was also here that he got to know a girl who was studying in the town, and began living with her.

He went on writing stories at night, but after he had written about fifty he realized he didn't like them. He thought that only in the desert or close to death was it worth writing something.

So, he set off for the Cévennes and camped in a cave in the mountains. He went down to the nearest village for provisions twice a week, and the rest of the time he spent filling notebooks with jottings on all that he saw around him, both the most commonplace and the most unusual things.

In the cave, he had an attack of lumbago which almost completely immobilized him, and a cold which made him keep on sneezing. He wrote a letter to his girlfriend in order to explain how it was impossible to describe appearances; he said that words are made of a different substance, and that there is no way of relating what appearances tell you. Moreover, up there, any story whatever seemed to him to be false.

One day, he went down to the nearest town and threw his books full of notes into the first litter bin he found. Then he took a train home.

At home, he found a short message in which his girlfriend announced she had gone away. He waited three months for her return, mostly in bed due to the lumbago and bronchitis he had contracted in the mountains.

One year after that, he had taken up his job at the garage again, he had enrolled at the University of Montpellier, and he was confined to bed by rheumatism of the spine. One afternoon, the girl who had left came back, saying she wanted to live with him.

After a further year, his child had been born, he was on the point of finishing university, and the girl was working as a librarian at a scientific institute.

And one day, the girl left her job and travelled right across France on foot as far as Brittany. She then made her way back and got to know a small band of Jews who used to raise horses, migrating with them through the pasture lands of southern France.

The men in that band believed that the human world was about to come to an end. They read the Bible everyday, and wanted to have nothing to do with the organized life of the city nor with its industry and commerce. The girl stayed with them. She had learnt to look after horses and accompanied the others in their migration.

They were in the Larzac region. One morning, when the girl had gone to buy provisions in a nearby village, all the men in this band were killed by machine-gun. Some people think it was the work of a Nazi commando unit that carried out military exercises in the area; in fact, men in camouflage had been seen doing firing practice in a deserted valley.

When the girl returned home, she had facial paralysis. After all that had happened, the man who wanted to write stories never managed to write anything again.

A scholar's idea of happy endings

The son of a chemist was studying abroad. On his father's death, he returned home to look after the dispensary, becoming the chemist of a small village on the outskirts of Viadana in the province of Mantua.

Word of his learning had spread in the country areas, fed by rumours about his huge library, about his prodigious cure for ear-ache, his ultra-modern method for irrigating the fields, and his fluency in twelve languages, not to mention rumours that he was translating the *Divine Comedy* into German.

The owner of a cheese-making factory in the area decided to pay a stipend to the scholar, who was by now middle-aged, in return for which he would help his daughter with her grammar school education. The girl, a sporting type, was not doing too well at school and, furthermore, she hated books, Latin, and good Italian prose. The chemist accepted — more from love of learning than for any financial motive — and every day for a whole summer he went to give lessons to the young athlete.

And one day it happened that the young athlete fell in love with him — so much so that she dropped all sport in favour of writing poetry, Latin verse and, of course, long letters.

There are still people who talk of the car the chemist bought to mark the occasion, the couple's long country trips, and even of noctural liaisons in a barn.

At any rate, evidence of their late-summer affair only came

to light the following winter when a bundle of letters was confiscated by the nuns at the girl's convent school, and duly handed over to her parents. The contents of these letters seemed so disgusting in the eyes of the owner of the cheese-making factory that he decided to ruin the chemist, and drive him from the village forever.

The girl's brothers, who were active fascists at the time, ransacked his shop on the village square a number of times, and on one occasion gave its owner a savage beating.

However, all this does not seem to have unduly worried the chemist. For a while, he continued to receive customers in the ransacked pharmacy, surrounded by broken window panes, torn down shelves and smashed jars. Then, one fine day, he shut up shop and withdrew among his books, rarely venturing out.

All the village knew him to be deep in his studies, and every now and again they saw him smiling as he crossed the square and headed for the post office to pick up new books that had arrived for him.

Some time later, he was taken to hospital and then to a sanatorium. He remained for a number of years in the sanatorium, and no one heard any more about him.

On his return from the sanatorium, the ageing scholar was extremely thin. An old housemaid, who had gone back to taking care of him, complained to everyone that he never wanted to eat: he said he didn't care to eat, and spent the whole day immersed in his books.

Thinner by the day, the man seldom went out and evidently no longer recognized anyone in the village, including the daughter of the now deceased owner of the cheese-making factory who he occasionally met in the square. Yet he smiled at all and sundry, and it is said he used to greet dogs by raising his hat.

Apparently, he had given up eating altogether after his old housemaid died and persisted in fasting for weeks on end, so that when he was found dead in his library (by a plumber) he was a skeleton in all but name: all that remained of him was wrinkled skin clinging to bones.

He was bent over the last page of a book onto which he was sticking a strip of paper.

Years later, his large library was inherited by a niece. The niece, rummaging through the books, believed she had worked out how the old scholar had spent the last part of his life.

For this man, every story, novel, or epic poem had to end happily. He obviously couldn't bear tragic endings, nor for a story to end on a sad or melancholic note. So, over the years, he devoted himself to re-writing the endings of some hundred or so books in every conceivable language. By inserting small sheets or strips of paper over passages that had to be re-written, he utterly changed the outcome of the stories, bringing them unfailingly to a happy ending.

Many of the last days of his life must have been dedicated to re-writing the eighth chapter of the third part of Madame Bovary, which is where Emma dies. In the new version, Emma recovers and is reunited with her husband.

His very last piece of work, however, consisted of the strip of paper he had in his fingers and which, on the point of dying of starvation, he was sticking onto the last line of a French translation of a Russian novel. This was possibly his masterpiece; by changing just three words, he transformed a tragedy into a satisfactory resolution of life's problems.

Ghosts at Borgoforte

There is a road at Borgoforte, in the province of Mantua, that runs along the bank of the Po as far as the point where the river Oglio joins the Po, and just here, on the Oglio, there is one of the very few floating bridges to survive from the great number that once existed in this area.

That road does not have tarmac, except for one initial stretch. In the surrounding area, there are many old farmhouses in ruins, and others still intact but no longer inhabited, and it is rare to come across anyone on this road after sunset, especially in the winter months when the stony track along the river is enveloped by banks of fog.

One November evening, two women who worked in the same office were going home along this road, and it was pouring with rain. The track on the embankment was lit only by their car headlights. All of a sudden, a boy (more a child, really) sprang into view on the edge of the embankment, where he was thumbing a lift in the beating rain.

In the few seconds between the apparition of the child at the top of the embankment and the moment the car stopped to give him a lift, the women had time to express their surprise on a number of counts. First of all because they lived locally and knew almost all the inhabitants of the area, and yet they had never before set eyes on that child lost in the night. And then because it seemed strange to them that the child was outside in the rain without a mac or overcoat, and that he was wearing only a striped summer top and shorts, and this in the month of November.

However, once he had got into the car and was sitting on the back seat, the child reassured them by talking quite freely. He explained that he'd gone for a bike ride along the river Oglio, and had found himself the wrong side of the floating bridge in the rain and with nowhere to take cover. So, he had crossed back over the bridge and abandoned the bicycle under the embankment, thinking it best to get a lift home in a car.

He said he was twelve, what his name was, where he went to school, what job his father did and the name of the farm where he lived. When the woman asked why it was they'd never seen him around, he replied he didn't know.

The two friends accompanied him to a place deep in the countryside much further on than they had to go themselves. Coming into sight of some houses, the child said they could stop, he lived right there, just down the track. He thanked the women, opened the car door and ran out into the rain, disappearing immediately down the track.

It was then that one of the two friends drew attention to something else. She drew the other woman's attention to the fact that, when he had got out of the car, the child didn't appear to be in the least bit wet — neither his clothes, nor his face nor his hair. It struck her that she had also seen this when they had picked him up in the beating rain, but it was only now that she gave it any thought. The other woman thought she had seen the same thing, and so they both felt the back seat where the child had been sitting.

However much they pressed, they could find no trace of water or dampness, not even on the floor of the car.

At this point — there in the rain and in the middle of a deserted road — the women were seized by panic. Without wasting a second they went straight to the house they lived in with the husband of the older woman, who was also the younger one's cousin.

For some reason they didn't dare tell the man what had happened. The next day was a Sunday and they went back to the cluster of houses where they had dropped the child off, and ascertained that not one of the inhabitants there knew anything about their passenger.

No one in that or any other farm in the surrounding countryside had ever seen or heard of a child resembling the one given a lift by the two women. Everyone listened to their tale and shrugged their shoulders. Someone suggested that maybe he was an outsider, and went to check whether he had stolen anything of theirs.

Nor for that matter did the police in Cesole, Campitello, Borgoforte and Serraglio find a trace of the child or his family when searching through their records. What's more, returning home one evening, the women discovered that the floating bridge on the river Oglio had not been open for a month because flooding had made it unstable and dangerous. Their passenger could not, therefore, live on the other side of the river.

The husband of the older woman got to know about the story when he heard it mentioned in a bar, and went and had a row with the two of them. According to him, the child had come from Borgoforte, perhaps with the intention of breaking into some of the houses at the bottom of the embankment which were always empty, except in the summer months.

However, as far as the women were concerned, the child had spoken as though he were telling the truth, and they stuck to this opinion. This, together with the episode of the traces of water they had never managed to find, made the husband wild with anger. He said things like that just couldn't happen, and that the women had therefore had an 'hysterical hallucination', perhaps because they were always going on about wanting to have children.

After Christmas, the older woman left her husband and went to live with the other woman in a cottage just outside Borgoforte, near the bridge on the Po. The husband didn't give the two women any peace for several months, turning up at night without warning and shouting at them each time that they were mad. However, he was then sent away on a trip by his company, and didn't go round there for some time.

One night the younger of the two had a dream about the child standing on the same embankment and in the company of people dressed in clothes from another era, maybe forty years earlier. It is only because she had to turn to someone to help her ascertain the date of the clothes that she mentioned it to a librarian from Mantua.

Perhaps the women thought that they had understood something from the dream; which is why they went back a couple of times to talk to the librarian about it.

The librarian from Mantua had had the impression that they regarded their own existence as something of little consequence. It seemed to him that they regarded themselves merely as 'tracks or channels for images' (the librarian's own words) — points through which images would pass which one often could not identify, like those in dreams, like many images from everyday life, or like images from another period in time such as the one of the child that, for some unknown reason, it had been their lot to see.

According to the librarian, the child had appeared to them as if he were — in their own words — a segment of time that comes back in a spiral of recurrence and which no one takes any notice of because each of us only recognizes his own images and blindly believes only in his own existence.

They were calm, and not unhappy. They explained their ideas to him in simple terms.

A nurse who was considered to be a medium went to call on them. She had come to ask the two women to take part in a séance so as to call up the ghost of the child. The younger woman started shouting that he wasn't a ghost. The nurse put the question: 'Well, if he isn't a ghost, what is he?' At which, the two asked her to leave.

Then the younger one had a breakdown. She had to be taken to hospital, and when the librarian from Mantua went to visit her, she didn't want to talk much about what had happened to her.

They were living on the ground floor of a small house at the top of a slope that ran down to the river bank — where there is a boatyard for repairing motorboats under the arches of the big bridge over the Po. From the living-room window they could see a restaurant on the slope which was always full of people in the evenings, so that there was a coming-and-going of cars and mopeds till late at night. Under the window there was a small orchard with flowers which was looked after by the landlord.

I can't begin to imagine what the women felt when, one evening, turning to the window, they saw the child on the other side of the pane looking at them. It was then that the younger one had the breakdown which she didn't want to talk about any more.

From the airports

For a long time now he had been without a language of his own in which to speak and write. A job done using only technical words in a foreign language — in a continent in which he had never managed fully to understand what others were saying — had given his face its distinctive contours and his voice its slow music. Since he had survived the person who had shared his travels and his life, he had decided one day to return to the continent he came from, only to discover that he was most at home in airports where he at last felt that he was in the company of others with the same purpose as himself.

He too was considered by many experts as an authoritative expert in something. However, he had often wanted recognition not for the specialist formulas that he used to teach others, but rather for the obscure and mundane work through which he had contributed to sustaining the age-old con-trick that was his science, picking his way through facts that weren't facts, evidence that wasn't evidence, and explanations that explained only themselves, and finally making it all add up thanks exclusively to the precision of the terms employed. When he was in the other continent, he had often wanted them to applaud him for this, and be able to take a bow in front of the public for being a performer who manipulated appearances in fabulous style, smiling to himself over his own act of deception in playing the part of the recognized scientist.

By this time, he was living in an old farmhouse that someone had modernized before he moved in. Waking up early in the morning, he often used to try to calculate the immense space he had around him, picturing the flat expanse of the plain where he lived as if seeing it from high above, and seeing to the east the succession of roads and landscapes as far as the sea's edge. The habit of running outside and looking at the sky the moment he woke up had for years set the tone of each day, and, as the years went by, the desire to run outside and look at the sky and the early morning stars over the fields came to him earlier and earlier. Waking up so early didn't strike him as a form of senile insomnia, but simply as a desire to look at the stars before starting his day. He used to say that they regulated his breathing and allowed him to devote himself to his studies without feeling they were utterly useless.

When the sun was up and light poured into the house, things he had been studying for years suddenly appeared definitive and self-evident, just like all the definitive and systematic arguments which for him were merely 'bad examples'. He used to say that the instant the sun came through a window, the floor tiles and chairs and kitchen table became nothing more than 'his objects'. From then on, everything appeared definitive, self-evident, unbearable; unbearable the boots in the hallway, the car (not his) for years parked in front of the house, not to mention the trees which still stood mocking him because he was not the natural scientist he was taken for and didn't even know their names.

That is why, once the sun was up, he would abandon his studies, leave the house and set off on one of his walks in the country — the kind of walk that lone walkers take. But sometimes, before going out, he would address the things in the house, especially the floor tiles in the kitchen, which seemed to be there just to confirm one particular idea he had of himself. He told the tiles: 'I'm not your owner even if it is my eyes looking at you. It's a waste of time fawning on me every morning with such familiarity, because the paths we follow will never meet.'

Almost fleeing into the open, he left behind a house that for him had become an environment made not of walls and fences but of images he had of himself — images that gave things an aura and an appearance of durability. At such times, the dirt road and the open land, the fields under cultivation, an abandoned country cemetry, they too were places full of images — the rich variety of the world which always made him want to take notes. And there, within sight of a motorway that crossed this flat terrain, he found land overrun with weeds which always caught his attention wherever he saw them growing — nettles, dock, spike grass, wild thistles, darnel, chick weed, glasswort, which comes from the steppes — in their separate colonies alongside old cardboard packing, lumps of brick, metal tailings and other refuse.

In his opinion, these plants didn't fawn before his eyes. Located in the waste ground of every continent and in places where the soil and air are more acidic, along with all the other 'objects' that belong to someone or other, for him they would always conjure up the idea of another world from which he felt himself excluded.

Nor in the fog did the distant trees — the lines of poplars, cypresses, mulberries — and houses along the mist-enveloped embankment seem to fawn before his eyes; they didn't ask to be recognized as a part of his world of images to remember and treasure.

This is why he used to say that when he found himself on foggy days on the top of an embankment, he managed to think things that he could never have thought when doing his job. While the solitude filling his body in such moments let him forget his various shortcomings in getting along according to other people's expectations of him, it also allowed him to imagine everything that exists out there — things, phenomena, populations — as linked by processes finely spun by thought, by the endless minutiae, the endless stories, told and untold, that seemed to him to hold together a seamless web in the emptiness of the planet.

With these ideas in his head and enclosed by a cloud of mist, he was sometimes overcome with euphoria. Because it seemed to him at such moments that being there on that embankment was like being everywhere. The seamless web, of which he too was a part, was always with him, in his body and in his mind.

He used to say that, from the time they had operated on his nose to remove a cyst, he had lost his sense of smell and become more rational. And he had recently become a little deaf as well and that had helped make him more rational. Perhaps only by losing some of one's senses does one become more rational, he used to say. For example, only now that he was without a sense of smell had he begun to think about the smells of the seasons, and to conceive of them as a good means of finding one's bearings in the world, better than a compass.

He said he had never been able to see anything within himself nor for that matter anything outside himself; too anxious when young and in middle age, wanting always to move onto something new, he had failed to recognize his own limitations. Now he saw that his limitations had become the path he had to follow — a path laid down by his infinite inability to do anything different. He had lived in the United States and Canada for thirty-odd years and had never learnt to speak English with a local accent nor ever learnt the language properly. He liked accents because they always used to make him smile, but anybody could tell from his accent that he was a man who didn't belong anywhere in the world.

Stars always filled him with a sense of wonder. There was both a constancy and inconstancy in the distant stars that for him was quite beyond our grasp. All the names men had given to things, places, plants, and ways of living and feeling — all that, for him, represented the Misery of History and was nothing but a tiny element of inconstancy. Equally ridiculous were the petty fakers like him ('modern', scientific fakers), who searched for an element of constancy through the abstraction of the names they gave to things — the 'new' names, the 'technical' names, the names of places everyone referred to as if to something precise, the adjectives and the adverbs. In his eyes, only verbs seemed sufficiently rigorous, even when thinking about the stars.

From the time he became a little deaf, the system of giving names to things appeared to him to be a gross and demented fabrication, like the principles of his science, like the abstraction of a single planetary God, the abstraction of money, and many other abstractions. In contrast, the accents and intonations of speech he heard in the bars and shops where he went to buy things were now a memory for him in his deafness — a music belonging to situations that were constantly changing according to the hour and the place and the people present, which often made him linger, glad to be with others waiting for time to pass.

He could not share in that music of the shops and bars because he no longer had a language of his own in which to speak. However, when he replied to a question, he was grateful they had asked because it meant he could remain with other people a moment longer.

When he woke up early in the morning, it often seemed to him that he was in the far north, in an icy region. He had cold feet and it was like being in a bivouac alone in the snow, and he couldn't decide whether to get out of his sleeping-bag and run and look up at the dawn sky. I must be getting ill, he would think.

Yet later on, when pissing against those trees in front of the house, and paying back their perpetual mockery of him, he used to think that maybe he had stayed alive too long. And some autumn mornings, setting out on one of his walks — the kind lone walkers take — he reached a raised point above the flat land where he sometimes managed to imagine that he was on the outer edge of the planet and that he was setting off towards a time when his experience would turn into silence.

He used to say that leaving the other continent he had felt especially at home in airports. Whenever he watched the passengers through the glass partition setting off in a line towards the aeroplane, they appeared to him each time like evacuees who were choosing to undertake the journey only because, for them, like him, there was nothing left to do or say on his side of the glass, and, like him, they were already resigned to their fate as eternal travellers or tourists.

Meteorites from outer space

The woman says that at one time she couldn't stand people's lack of generosity. Now she doesn't think about it any more, but it seems to her that, generally speaking, women are more generous than men, and old people more generous than young people, except when they are stupid and embittered.

Many years earlier she had had to cut short her veterinary studies, and for a long while she had not wanted to go out of the house because everyone seemed to her so lacking in generosity. In the end, and after much pressure, her relations succeeded in taking her to a psychiatrist in Modena, a youngish doctor whose hair, however, had gone almost completely white.

Before talking to the doctor, she had wanted to look at him closely to see what sort of person he was, and she had asked him to stand in the middle of the room to let himself be inspected. The doctor consented, and she circled around inspecting him.

Then, she asked him to take off his jacket to see how he carried his shoulders. The doctor consented to this as well, smiling and then asking: 'How do you find me?'

She told him: 'I find you handsome, but also a little sad, because you don't trust other people.' She saw from the way he carried his shoulders that he didn't trust other people, and asked him how he could treat people if he didn't trust them. The doctor replied gravely: 'You're right, but I'm not to blame.'

At any rate she had agreed to talk to him, seeing that he'd

consented to let himself be looked at, and this meant that he was at least a little generous.

The doctor asked her why she never wanted to go out of the house, and she replied: 'I don't want to go out because people aren't a bit generous and pass too many judgements.' The doctor explained that one needed to make an effort to forget that other people were passing judgements, otherwise one would be paralysed, and she said: 'Yes, I know, but I'm ugly, and for me it's harder to forget.'

At the end of the visit, the young doctor with the white hair made two prophesies. The first, that one day she would realize that she was just like everyone else because she too passed judgements on others, and anyway staying shut up at home meant she wasn't a bit generous either; the second, that in the space of a year something would happen that would shake her and make her forget these problems.

The two prophesies came true. The second came true first, and the other came true subsequently and as a consequence of the first.

One day she was busy tidying the orchard and saw, in the sky, a ball of fire looping upwards. Then, the ball did a zig-zag with two bangs and made a downward loop, ending up in a field beyond her house.

She ran into the field and found a hole from which smoke was rising. There was a rim of earth around the hole, and when she touched it, she scalded her hand. Her hand felt scalded for a month, but there was no trace of burning to be found.

Her father, who had heard the whistling noise and the bangs, rushed over thinking it might be a bomb dropped inadvertently by some passing plane. Then her brother's son arrived as well, explaining that it must be a meteorite, and then her father wanted to ring up a journalist in Modena straightaway to get him to write an article about the meteorite that had fallen into his field.

She stayed there a long time looking at the hole in the field from which smoke had now stopped rising, and she saw there were some fragments of rock inside. She scooped them up with a shovel, and put them into a small plastic bucket.

When the journalist arrived, the first thing he wanted to know was: 'Has there been any metal fusion?', and she showed him the fragments of rock. The journalist said there hadn't been any metal fusion, and so it was a meteorite of no interest, because lots of meteorites that land on earth are just rock, but a few contain metal, and that's what counts.

Her father, who had counted on becoming famous because the meteorite had fallen in his field, was left thoroughly disillusioned. She, however, had been greatly shaken at seeing that fiery globule appear in the sky, and hoped that the doctor's prophesy (the second one) would come true.

The morning after she had found the rock fragments on the ground, the bottom of the plastic bucket had melted. The fragments were radioactive, and passing her hand over them stung. So she put them in glass jars, the ones used for jam, and put these jars in the outhouse.

And then some things happened that made a deep impression on her. The first was that her brother's son and a cousin of hers, one fine day, were going to make love in the outhouse as they often did in the afternoons (in obedience to their youthful impulses), when they felt their legs stinging, and the stinging lasted two weeks. Then one day she found the cat rubbing itself against the wall because its back was stinging. And yet another day, there was a dove which was trembling on the window of the outhouse, and, finally, two rats which had bitten away their feet, because they had obviously gone too near the jars and had become contaminated.

Almost without realizing it, she got in the car (she hadn't driven for years), and went to Revere and then to Ostiglia, to find some books that might explain where meteorites come from. It struck her as amazing that those fragments of rock came from outer space and perhaps from the stars, and she suspected that the radioactivity had penetrated her as well, sucking her towards something that frightened her a little, but also attracted her more than anything else could. So, because she was thinking only about these things, she had failed to notice that she had gone out of the house and back among people without paying any attention to their judgements of others and their lack of generosity.

After a few weeks, she took a train and went to the young doctor with the white hair to tell him that his prophesy (the second one) had come true. She told him that perhaps her soul had been attracted to something outside her that had existed before she was born, but she couldn't tell what it was. That is why she had stopped thinking about her earlier problems.

The doctor was very gratified by these developments and advised her, in order to complete her recovery, to buy herself some new clothes. He said that when one puts on new clothes, one feels like another person, and this would do her good.

Not long afterwards, the woman went to a boutique in Modena to buy a dress and other clothes to replace the ones she used to wear when shut up at home. Going around in her new clothes she felt as if she were another woman, who was at once herself and not herself.

In fact, it so happened that in putting on her new clothes she had suddenly become beautiful, and therefore she was no longer herself but another woman. Many were of the opinion that she had become beautiful, including the men of Revere, who now found her fascinating and, when they saw her, sought to court her.

Wherever she went, she would look at this other woman from the outside. She observed her talk, greet people, go into shops, answer questions in the way one ought, and make all the right faces — and all with effortless ease. Little by little, she began to understand that the other woman would pass judgements on everyone and would only say things she had heard others say, although she always said them as if she had thought them herself, and hence her effortless ease. In the end, she came to the conclusion that the other woman said and did everything in exactly the same way as other people, that other people did and said things in exactly the same way as this woman who was almost identical to her, and who was perhaps a kind of automaton.

However, seeing that the other woman got along well with other people, and, what's more, that they all found her fascinating, she let her get on with it.

She wrote to the doctor to tell him that his first prophesy had also come true in that she had finally realized that she (that is to say, if not she then the other woman who did everything in her place) was identical to all the other people. She also sent him a poem she had composed, to thank him for his help.

Many months passed. One summer's day, the young doctor went to call on her in her house in the country near Revere, and then the woman asked him what he thought of the poem she had composed for him.

The doctor said: 'It's a strange poem — bizarre and difficult at the beginning, and, in contrast, simple and natural at the end. It's like your life, which was bizarre and difficult in its early stages, and has got better and will get better gradually as you grow old, as often happens with people who have had a troubled youth.'

This was the doctor's third prophesy, and this too came true over the years, simply with the passing of the days and the months and the thoughts that come to mind.

The young doctor, who had been in love with her for some time, for she was a fascinating woman, asked her, one fine day, if she would marry him. She consented, seeing that from the very start he had at least shown a little generosity.

She is now fifty-two, has a daughter, and all is well with her. She says that, growing old, one learns not to take too much notice of that automaton who does everything for us, who talks when one should talk, returns greetings when greeted, and laughs when it is appropriate to laugh. Since our souls are more and more attracted to something outside us, then (if one's not stupid or embittered), we also learn to stop believing the words and thoughts of that other who deals with people for us. We learn to find all our judgements ridiculous, and to make fun of them when talking to ourselves. So, by talking a lot to ourselves, we too can become more generous.

The city of Medina Sabah

A young man from Mirandola, in the province of Modena, had studied to be an engineer. When he became an engineer, he was given a job in a factory that made lifts and very soon was sent to Africa to install and test a lift system in a government building.

He left, and following his departure nothing was heard of him for three years. When he came back, he sold his father's farm and set up a small factory. However, he never wanted to talk about what had happened to him in Africa nor say which countries he had seen.

One day he decided to get married, and the bride's father said to him: 'I used to know your father and I'm happy you're marrying my daughter, but I will only give my consent when you tell me what happened to you in Africa.'

The young man replied that he would tell him his story but only on the day of the wedding and not before, and so it was to be. During the wedding feast he recounted what had happened to him in Africa.

He had loaded two lorries with the equipment to be installed and was travelling down a long, straight road near the frontier. With him there was a Yoruba guide who gave him information on everything they saw.

They had stopped just outside a village and could hear some music in the distance. He, the Yoruba guide and two Wolof lorry drivers set off on foot towards the music. They were met in a small street by native women, who invited them into a house and served them with things to eat and drink.

They stayed in this place for a week, served by the native women on the patio of a large wooden house from which they could clearly hear the sound of music both night and day. They ate and drank, and in the evening they would go and explore the streets of the town. He used to ask his Yoruba guide: 'But where are we?' The guide answered: 'We are in the city of Medina Sabah,' but would not to tell him more.

In the streets, there were gangs of children running around, shouting and singing, and the guide explained that the children invent almost all the songs. Then he explained: 'The orchestra of the Big Mamma which you can hear in the distance is made up of fifty women who play all the instruments and is directed by the Big Mamma who is ninety years old. Every day, the children shouting invent new songs, which the orchestra of the Big Mamma then play on their fifty instruments. People also come to record them and introduce their music throughout the whole world.'

When he asked to see the big women's orchestra, he was told he couldn't. Sitting on the patio of the house, he could listen to the music non-stop day and night, and eat and drink without spending a thing. However, he could not go and see the orchestra of the Big Mamma.

After a week he left his companions and went back to the road on foot. Here he found that all that remained of the two lorries were their cabins and some empty packing cases. Everything else had been stolen.

When he arrived in the capital, he reported the theft and was immediately put in prison, because the equipment to be installed was government property and he was responsible for it.

In prison, where he remained for over a year, he made friends with a Bandial storyteller, who was in prison because he had refused to accept state cooperatives taking over his crops. He had come to the capital to talk with the cooperative managers, but two policemen had immediately arrested him.

This man explained to the engineer the fundamental difference between storytellers like himself, and the *griot*, who apparently told tales about people's ancestral origins.

The Bandial storytellers don't trust the *griots*, because, according to them, they are all fakers and invent the genealogies whether of families or heads of state; they make people pay in advance and invent what they like. And since they invent what they like, they grow powerful.

Storytellers, on the other hand, don't invent what they like, and have to stick to what history tells them. A storyteller cannot be asked: 'But is your story true?' Because that would be a great insult. They narrate precisely what history tells them, not what they themselves invent.

One day, in the prison corridor, the Bandial storyteller saw a *griot* of the Diola people, and he recognized him at once because he could spot a *griot* instantly, even if he saw him from a distance. He shouted at him: 'Hey, *griot*, I can see you!' and the *griot* ran away and hid in shame.

The storyteller knew all there is to know about Medina Sabah. He told the engineer how it is a regular occurrence for lorry drivers to arrive along that road with lorries full of rice or groundnuts, for them to come to a stop under the spell of the music, and, enticed by the music, for them to be received by the women. The women offer them palm-wine to drink and fish and rice to eat for days on end, and when the lorry drivers return to the road their load has disappeared, and the lorries are without their engines and without wheels.

The storyteller also used to say that there are some lorry drivers who know all too well what they are letting themselves in for when setting foot in Medina Sabah. They know that they will later finish up in prison for losing their load and their lorry. However, nothing would make them give up the delights of following that music and being waited on by the women, all the while listening to the orchestra of the Big Mamma in the distance.

The Bandial storyteller confirmed that all the songs were invented by the children who play in the streets. However, unlike other villages, this one has the orchestra of fifty women who collect and play the songs so that anyone can listen to them day or night. And the managers of the most famous musical groups go and record these songs which fill the air. Then, a famous singer makes a record of them, and appropriates the music.

There are singers who have become so famous and powerful in this way that they can challenge the governments. There is one who is more powerful than any other rock star in the entire world, and he built himself a huge fortress where the police cannot enter, where the people live according to his laws and where he can condemn to death whoever he wants.

This is the great power of the songs that first attract lorry drivers and then spread throughout the world.

When the groom finished telling his story at the wedding feast, nobody knew what to say and there was a long embarrassed silence. The next day a friend asked him why he had waited such a long time before revealing what had happened to him in Africa. The storyteller replied that he couldn't stand the chatter at wedding feasts, and that by holding the story back for the right occasion he felt sure he would shut everyone up.

The girl from Sermide

At Sermide there was at one time a floating bridge which crossed the Po and led to a factory whose chimney bricks were still unblackened. One day this factory had to close down and one of its managers disappeared without a trace. The man had a daughter to whom, before disappearing, he had left in his will a house and the income from other landed property. A number of years later his wife died and his daughter moved to a city in order to study at the university. Here she met a student with curly hair and began living with him.

They lived in a small flat together with a third student, who was extremely thin. The student with curly hair used to go around all day making political speeches in bars, at the university, or at factory gates. The girl from Sermide used to neglect her studies, maintaining that she learnt much more from the speeches of the student with curly hair. So she followed him around, listening to him speak all the time; otherwise she would wait for him at home asleep.

As there came a time later on when nobody wanted to hear political speeches any more but the student carried on making them anyway, a number of people told him he had better shut up or go and do his talking somewhere else.

So he and the girl from Sermide decided to look for a more hospitable environment for their ideas and moved to the capital. However, it was impossible to find a flat there, and the two of them had to go and live as the guests of someone from the same city as the student.

The student got in touch with a screenwriter who had written many screenplays and with various high-ups who were prepared to help him find work in the film business, to return a favour from his father. With a screenplay ready and the government grant promised by these high-ups due to arrive any day, he decided to start shooting the film straightaway.

The film had to be a low-budget one; a real life story with two characters who would talk politics the whole of the time.

A bank made a loan, with the girl's house at Sermide as collateral. So the student was able to make a start on his film.

On the sixth day of shooting the money ran out and a further loan, made with some reluctance by the bank, was scarcely enough to pay off the technicians. Then one night the film equipment that they had hired was stolen and the following day the high-up people informed the student that the government grant had been frozen.

However, by way of recompense, they offered him the possibility of making a documentary about some underdeveloped areas in the south of Italy.

He and the girlfriend from Sermide made a preliminary visit to an underdeveloped area, where they discovered the existence of unknown local crafts. On returning to the capital, they decided to open a shop to sell and publicize these unknown local wares of which they had acquired a number of samples: terracotta whistles, statuettes, fire-crackers, and bowls and spoons made of wood.

When he found his house packed with samples of unknown crafts — samples which took up an entire corridor and blocked the way — their host asked the two of them to look for a flat of their own and take their stuff away as soon as possible.

And that is how, while going around the city in search of a house to rent, the student with curly hair discovered a splendid aristocratic apartment in semi-derelict condition which was on offer for a paltry sum.

He suggested to the girl that she sell her house in Sermide in order to purchase the apartment, with the aim of then re-selling it as soon as possible for an astronomical figure. Around the same time, however, the executors of the girl's estate told her that her properties would have to be sold in order to pay off the heavy mortgages that had built up over the years. The girl should return to Sermide at once.

The student, left to his own devices in the capital, got to know a young American countess who loved rock music. He proposed that she back and organize a series of concerts with the world's most famous bands in villages in the underdeveloped areas he had visited. As the American countess was much taken by the idea, the student went back to city in the north to get in touch with some friends who worked for a record company.

He stayed in the city three days. On the first day, he met someone just back from Provence who spoke to him about Provençal wool. He made an agreement with him to set up an import company for Provençal wool at the earliest opportunity.

The second day, he met an old political comrade who proposed shooting a documentary on the liberation movement in Baluchistan. And he, of course, agreed to the idea, and fixed a date for their departure.

Finally, on the third day, he met the extremely thin student with whom he had lived for some time, and the latter confided that he had in his possession several million lire.

The previous summer he had gone to work in a motorway toll booth. A lorry had run into the toll booth, completely destroying it and putting the thin student in hospital for several months with all his bones broken. Subsequently an insurance company had paid him compensation of several million lire.

The student with curly hair immediately put a proposal to his friend to double his capital in a week. He explained how, and the thin student agreed to the proposal. The two of them left the next day for Holland with the aim of buying a large second-hand foreign car, driving it back to Italy and re-selling it at a handsome profit.

In Holland, they bought an old Jaguar, and during the return journey, overheated the engine. They had to stay in Germany for a week waiting for the engine to be rebuilt. They spent a few million lire on rebuilding the engine and on the cost of the journey home. They got back to Italy and the next day the car was confiscated by the police for being illegally imported.

The thin student was charged and had to pay a nine million lire fine. Thus he lost his whole capital in precisely twelve days, starting from the moment he had bumped into the student with curly hair in the street.

In the meantime, the girl from Sermide had sold her house. Nothing remained of her property or income. She had to pay off debts to the bank, the scriptwriter, and the hire company for its film equipment which had been stolen.

All that now remained to be done was to purchase the spacious aristocratic apartment with the proceeds from the sale of the house and carry out the restoration work, in order to then re-sell it for an astronomical figure and pay off all the debts.

Summer came. The student with curly hair left for the south with the young American countess who loved rock music to organize their concerts in the underdeveloped areas, and also because the two of them had in the meantime got engaged.

The girl from Sermide spent the summer in the spacious aristocratic apartment, sitting on the floor among the fallen beams, torn-up floors, mouldy walls and broken windows, reading novels and eating bread and apples.

It was early autumn when a telegram brought her news of the return of her father, who had disappeared without a trace many years earlier. During her return journey, she saw the fields of burnt stubble and the first fogs on the plains. She embraced her father once more, and told him the whole of her story. Her father listened to her and then said in a weak voice: 'May God forgive your innocence.'

The story of a carpenter and a hermit

There was a man who lived in Ficarolo, in the province of Ferrara, and was a carpenter. One evening, returning home by bicycle along a small road that leads to the village square, he was hit by a car driven by strangers — because he was pedalling too slowly. As there were two passengers in the car, and no other witnesses to the accident, it was easy for the driver to maintain that the cyclist had cut across him.

After some weeks in hospital, the carpenter goes to a solicitor for help at the trial. The solicitor, not hiding his doubts as to whether the carpenter's evidence on its own will be enough to win the case, proposes a settlement with the other party. The carpenter, however, first he does not understand even one half of the solicitor's objections, and, second, insists on his entitlement to full compensation. So, he dismisses the lawyer on the eve of the hearing and decides to go through with the trial alone.

He is therefore alone in court, maintaining that there is no need for solicitors as he is in the right and ought to receive compensation.

After various procedural objections and the summoning of a counsel for the defence, the moment finally arrives when the passengers of the car are called upon to testify. At this point, the carpenter, realizing that every word the witnesses have said is a lie, remains so dumbfounded he does not even want to speak to the counsel for the defence. And when, in the end, the judge asks him to give his version of events, he declares that he has nothing to say and everything's fine as it is.

Consequently, he is sentenced to pay damages for the accident and, in addition, the costs of the trial.

A few days later, he sells all his carpenter's tools to his assistant, who has long wanted to set up on his own, handing over his trading licence as well as his workshop. He goes back home and stays seated in a chair in the kitchen for a week, always answering his wife's questions the same way — his head's overheated and he can't talk to her.

The next week, he stays seated in a bar watching people as they go by in the square, and one evening, instead of returning home, he sets off from the village. He sets off on foot towards the banks of the Po. After a lot of walking, he arrives at daybreak at a hut where a hermit fisherman lives.

This hermit is an ex-racing driver who, on retiring from racing, opened a garage where sports car engines were 'suped up', and made more powerful. However, tiring of this work and in the light of reading a lot of psychology books, he had decided to become a fisherman hermit, and retreat to a hut on the banks of the Po.

The hermit's hut is made of sheet-metal and other salvaged materials. A panel above the door reads 'MICHELIN TYRES'.

The carpenter knows that the hermit has retreated to this hut because he doesn't want to speak to anyone ever again. So, on his arrival, he doesn't say a single word to him. He sits down and begins looking at the river.

It is summer, and for about a month the two of them go fishing together and sleep in the same hut in uninterrupted silence.

One morning, the carpenter wakes up and the hermit is no longer there, because he has gone to drown himself in the river, under the old Stellata bridge.

That day, the carpenter had the chance to witness, from a distance, the recovery of the hermit, who, as it happened, was a very good swimmer; wrapped in a blanket he was carried away by his wife in a large sports car, thus bringing his career as a hermit to an end.

The carpenter returned to the village and asked his assistant to employ him as an assistant in his old workshop. Which he did. The carpenter is still alive and has only just retired.

Crossing the plains

Over seventy years ago, around 1910, my mother crossed the plains on a cart, together with her brothers, various goods and chattels and her parents. The places she went through must have been full of marshes and it is possible that a great number of villages didn't even exist then. Where they didn't encounter marshes, they may have found retting pits for hemp or rice fields. The roads could not have been much more than tracks between the fields with mulberrries and elms, maybe the odd poplar, and perhaps stretches of holm and oak.

The journey must have taken all of a day and a night, or even longer. My grandfather and grandmother were tailors and had five children with them — three boys and two girls. My mother must have been seven or eight years old at the time.

When they reached the gates of the town, they would have crossed a fine square and seen the church and the tall clock-tower and the bridge over the canal.

On the other side of the bridge were thc walls and a gateway into the town, which shut at sunset like all town gates used to do, I imagine. Here, the customs men checked the wayfarers' goods. The customs men probably made them get down off the cart, to check there wasn't contraband among the goods.

Before letting them enter the town, the customs men had said: 'But what makes you come and live here? You're better off in the country. You lead a happy life there. Don't you know that in towns the air's bad, there's always a terrible din, and the sun never sets on the horizon?'

This is the only detail of the journey that I have heard recounted. One of my mother's sisters has repeated the story to me on three separate occasions, over a period of time, but always using the same words spoken in dialect by the customs men — words she remembers like a formula.

Apart from this, she remembers that on that evening, and many other evenings subsequently, my mother's three brothers kept an eye on the prospect of Porta Mare to see whether the sun would go down there.

In front of them must have been a long and rather wide street, with cobble stones and tiny houses on either side. As the windows were at road level, every house must have had grilles with different wrought-iron patterns. All the front doors must have been different from one another as well, even the small ones with a knocker in the middle or a bell-pull on the side.

The colours of the street facing them must all have been on the soft side with none of the bright colours that we are used to. There must have been subtle gradations of ochre and sepia and Siena red in the plaster of the houses, the colour of worn brick in a church, the dust-grey of the cobble stones at the very bottom of the street.

As evening fell, they would probably have seen people sitting outside their front doors. There couldn't have been much noise, I imagine, since all the inhabitants of the street were serious-minded artisans, like those in my mother's family, who used to talk without raising their voices. I imagine they would also have worn broadly cut rather then tight-fitting clothes. Then, I imagine there were people who would be walking down the middle of the street scattered in small groups, and children who'd be roaming around after dark.

At the mouth of the funnel created by this long street was the prospect, that is to say, the city walls and the gate called Porta Mare. And that's where one never got to see the sun set on the horizon.

After this journey, my mother fell ill, spent the whole night trembling and sweating, lost her hair and turned black all over. They took her to hospital where they treated her with kefir's medicine, which was a yoghurt used at the time as a disintoxicant.

The three brothers found work — one as a cobbler's assistant and the other two as apprentice carpenters. But it wasn't long before one of the two apprentice carpenters started to lay wooden floors.

Once, when telling this story, my aunt must have added that by the time my mother left hospital, her brothers had already explored every nook and cranny of the town. And that's how they finally managed to take her to see the sun set on the horizon, not at Porta Mare, which is to the east, but on the opposite side, to the west.

A celebrated occupier of cities

One night in the month of May in the year 1922, thousands of farmworkers set off from the areas around Codigoro, Massafiscaglia, Migliarino, Goro and Porto Garibaldi on a journey aboard large barges which were towed by horses on the river bank. Another army of farmworkers from numerous other villages began the trek to Ferrara at daybreak, going on foot, by bicycle and by cart. When morning came, those on the barges got off at the Arginale Ducale dock and entered the city together with the others.

The leader of this gathering was a shortish young man with a moustache and hair that formed two triangles on the sides of his skull. He was an ex-student, who had graduated in uniform during the war and still wore soldier's boots and breeches. He wore breeches baggy at the side, a band of silk around his waist, and a kerchief around his neck. When he spoke he made sweeping movements in the air with his hands.

It was compulsory at this time for large landowners to take on a certain number of unemployed for seasonal farm work — in the ratio of six persons per thirty hectares. From April until the end of the summer, these farmworkers went back to being unemployed. The government, in order to give them employment, usually earmarked a fixed sum per province for public works. No sum was earmarked for that year, so the city had been occupied to force the government to maintain spending on public works at the usual level.

That day the young man dressed as a soldier marched through the city at the head of the army of unemployed. He made many speeches and forced the prefect to telephone the minister to ask for an immediate commencement of public works. He got what he wanted and was applauded in the streets.

A week later, when he returned home to his small room to sleep — the kind of room typical of ex-students who live at home — he noted down how happy he was at the widespread recognition given his exploits in the papers and at the congratulations from the national leaders.

For him, occupying a city was now a straightforward matter. It was enough that he issued an order, that the order reached its destination and was relayed to others, and tens of thousands of people would be ready to move.

His orders consisted of notes written in bold handwriting that formed elongated ellipses at the top. Every order — complete with details of time-tables, meeting points and routes — was accompanied by stipulations of a moral nature, and concluded with exhortations to work hard, often with veiled threats aimed at those who didn't do their duty to the full. His signature consisted of a single stroke of the pen, which indicated a summary gesture.

Orders were entrusted to men on bicycles and the recipients had to send an immediate written reply, either via the same men on bicycles, or by other means. The surrounding countryside was completely flat and the distances not excessive. Only in an emergency did they send a messenger in a car.

He used to communicate with his leaders via letters many pages long, which were entrusted to members of the organization who travelled by train. He tended to digress in these letters, using numerous verbs in the future tense, and putting superlatives and exclamation marks all over the place. The leaders used to reply with type written letters in a more laconic vein.

In his letters to the leaders, he often alluded to new methods of penetrating areas not yet controlled by others. He sometimes peppered the notes he sent his subalterns with words of exhortation concerning such methods. These phrases were, on his orders, publicly displayed in the local headquarters of the organization. It is to him we owe a phrase which, for all its ambiguity, is still on display in certain banks.

The national leaders had put him in charge of an immense region. Under him he had heads of districts, who in turn were in command of local leaders, who in turn were in command of those in charge of groups, and each group comprised one thousand persons.

This is how, soon afterwards, he would effortlessly manage to occupy the city of B., and then the city of R., where a crowd had lynched a porter belonging to his organization.

A young man — standing in an open car, his hair blowing in the wind — would arrive one morning in R. to take revenge.

He would ask the police to intervene at the porter's funeral to avoid incidents between the conflicting parties. With this ruse, he would divert the entire police force then taking up position in the city, being able thereby, at his leisure, to occupy the headquarters of the opposition, a large hotel in the city centre. His adversary, a fat man who looked like a shopkeeper, is reported to have left the hotel in tears, between two lines of armed men.

That night, while he was persuading the prefect and police to forestall a show-down between the conflicting parties, his men would go and set fire to the headquarters of the agricultural cooperatives, which were opposed to his organization. Returning to the occupied hotel, he would contemplate the flames climbing into the darkness, and note that his men were in 'high spirits'.

The next day, he would borrow a column of lorries from the head of police to take his men out of the city before there were serious clashes. With the lorries, he'd scour the countryside, burning down cooperatives and political clubs, and seeking out the enemy in their homes and beating up a lot of people.

At night, after their exploits, he would stop out in the open country to gaze up at the stars.

The following week, he would draw up his army in person

outside the city of P., so as to occupy the part of the city the other side of the river where they had put up barricades. A young man wrappped in an old wartime cloak, though on this occasion wearing officer's boots and not soldier's leggings, would be seen standing looking into the distance at the city he hoped to take.

As the prefect had been unable to prevent the armed insurrection in the old quarter of the city, he planned to enter the city with his army on bicycles and give battle to the insurgents.

Would he manage to cross the bridge and storm the area on the other side of the river? No, he wouldn't. Instead, he would make way for the King's army, with due ceremony, standing to attention in front of a general who promised him he'd re-establish order as quickly as possible.

Before leaving the city, he would post up some proclamations explaining to the population that his men had rushed to defend the Values Enshrined in History. A great number of people, getting off the tram or cycling by, would not stop to look at these proclamations as it rained a lot during that period, even though it was late spring.

At the beginning of October, a young man in a uniform with officer's epaulettes is hiding from the police in a village near P. He is making preparations for the occupation and definitive subjugation of the areas on the other side of the river that are still in revolt. He issues orders to his officers and sends messages to the leaders of the organization. His army has to break through at various points on the other side of the river, evacuate women and children, seize all the insurgents' arms, and burn and raze to the ground a great number of houses.

On the other side of the river, there is a trade union leader who is dressed like a character from an adventure story; he too is wearing baggy trousers, boots and a silk band around his waist. The young man in officer's uniform can't wait to confront him.

Will he confront him? No, he won't, because he is dissuaded by a laconic letter from the his leaders. The whole organization will be mobilized for a more important purpose, and the following year the young man will have to give up occupying cities and return to his family, because of the absolute and unqualified success of the organization.

He will then write a fake diary recording this year of struggles, which scholars still make use of when recounting the stories of these great occupiers of cities and other important events in history.

Let us now leave our young man to write his fake diary. He is in good health, has a good appetite, doesn't suffer from insomnia at night, and, furthermore, he is also able to express in words an image he has created of himself.

The family tomb, which awaits him in the cemetery of Ferrara, is a large cask in black marble with grey veins, inside a chapel where an inscription in embossed letters spells out the family name. The chapel is surrounded by a box hedge, and two of the cemetery's gravel paths intersect at its left-hand corner. In the earth between the gravel and the box hedge, there's recently sprung up a strange wild plant that some people call *gar.* It is a small plant that, when rubbed, gives off the scent of garlic.

What is it, this natural life?

A story set in the area around Argenta, in the province of Ferrara. The son of a farmer who was studying to become a doctor of medicine had rented a small room in the city, in the house of a widow. It was here he often used to talk for hours to the widow's retarded son, explaining to him his philosophy.

The philosophy of the farmer's son went: if you aren't natural and don't do things naturally in the way that animals do, you might as well not exist. He personally didn't like over-formal people as they aren't natural, whereas he liked chemistry a lot as it is something natural.

His father's orchard produced apples and pears. However, there were too many apples and pears on the market at the time, and the orchard was no longer profitable.

The farmer's son thought his father was a phoney like the rest of the peasants, while the father was intimidated by a son who was at university. So, the two didn't talk much, but every now and again they yelled at each other.

The son shouted at the father that he was an ignoramus, incapable of even running his own affairs. And once, to prove it, he sold the entire crop of apples and pears for him — and that in the year the apples were ruined by hail and therefore unsellable.

The farmer's son bought a car and set off on a trip to get the money back from the wholesaler he'd sold the fruit to. He took with him a friend, who was a waterways official (he superintended the water levels in a canal basin), the widow's retarded son, plus the widow's other son who had just become a bookkeeper.

During the trip, the four of them stopped at regular intervals to eat and drink, and the farmer's son always offered to pay, because his philosophy went: if someone has money, he should share it with others. In the discussions during the trip, they elaborated on many of the ideas in this philosophy, especially the waterways official who frequently mentioned Jesus Christ.

At the end of the long trip which took them to the far south, they still hadn't managed to find the wholesaler. The latter, pursued by debts and bankruptcy notices, had made himself scarce.

They spent several days visiting deserted winter beaches, always at the expense of the farmer's son. Until, in an out-of-the-way hotel, they found the wholesaler.

This man fully concurred with the philosophy of the four others, and for some days he too was invited to eat and drink by the farmer's son, who then cancelled his debt, accepting the fact that the apples and pears had been ruined by the hail and were therefore unsellable.

By the time they parted, they were great friends. The farmer's son, to help the wholesaler out, even made him a loan, letting him have a cheque on his father's current account.

When the son returned from the long trip, the father explained to him that they were ruined.

After a further attempt to get through the medical exam that he always did badly in, the farmer's son decided to give up his studies and transform his father's orchard. His father had had a stroke and thereafter he no longer spoke; he lived separately in one room and kept himself to himself.

Since the apples and pears had stopped being profitable, the trees were cut down, and peach and apricot trees were planted in their place. The farmer's son tended the orchard but not long afterwards it happened that his girlfriend got pregnant, and he then abandoned everything and disappeared for a while.

Back in his rented room in the city, he explained to the widow's retarded son that he would never marry. First of all, because as far as he was concerned priests were a blot on the landscape, and then because getting married is the most unnatural thing there is.

Anyway, the abandoned fruit trees hadn't produced anything, and he had to return to his village to find work. Around this time, experts began to arrive looking for objects for museums of rural life, and the farmer's son had long discussions with them, because museums didn't seem natural things to him.

However, he gave away many of his father's old agricultural implements. And when he took them to see the room where his father slept like a peasant of bygone days — on an iron bedstead and mattress of maize leaves, with a bed-warming pan typical of peasants of old — the experts got extremely interested in these objects. So much so, that he handed them over and they immediately took them away.

That day, returning from a bicycle ride, the father could no longer find his bed. Without saying a word, he moved into the old hen house to sleep, taking his camp bed in with him. He bolted himself in and didn't come out again.

In the neighbouring village they had set up a building co-operative that also carried out property deals. The farmer's son was given a job and, as he knew how to express himself, he instantly got on well. He rented out the orchard, which he couldn't look after any longer, and, one fine day, they even elected him chairman of the cooperative.

It was then, one Sunday when they'd gone fishing, that he and the waterways official established once and for all that the true and natural life would be as follows: to live in total darkness and without hearing, because everything is phoney and everything is a racket. Indeed, the philosophy of the farmer's son didn't fit in with his cooperative's property deals. So he immediately resigned as chairman, and was then dismissed altogether.

He subsequently sold the entire farm, apart from the old barn where they stored the fruit and the adjoining hen-house with his father inside. With this money, his wife (the pregnant girlfriend he had married) opened a boutique in a nearby town.

In the barn that they had kept, he set up a kiln for producing ceramic ware. A lecturer at the School of Fine Art had supplied him with the patterns of the tableware used at one time by the dukes of the surrounding area. On the plates and bowls could be seen strange animals almost oriental or Persian in style.

The farmer's son decided, after consulting with the waterways official, to make perfect replicas of this antique tableware and export it throughout the world.

After producing a large quantity of cups and plates, copying not only the recurrent imperfections of form but also the wonderful patterns, the colours and the application of the colours in flecks that were superimposed on one another and overlapped the borders of the pattern, it dawned on him that this tableware didn't interest anyone. At best, he could sell the odd plate or cup to a connoisseur, but how many connoisseurs are there around?

His son has grown up. He now lives on the money his wife made in her boutique. He has begun dyeing his now rapidly greying hair.

He frequently talks about the Persian patterns on his tableware. For him, the patterns bring an infinity of questions to mind. Such as: At what hours of the day were these bowls used in the times of the dukes? What foods and what liquids did they hold? Who was the potter who made them? On looking around him while making them, what did the potter see? What stories were being told at the time of the Persian patterns which the potter was copying?

In these bowls there's a thread that links him to goodness knows how many potters and people going back to time immemorial. To him it seems strange that the eyes see none of this, they merely see an object.

My uncle discovers the existence of foreign languages

My grandfather on my father's side was a very thin, very short man of exactly the same height and born on the same day as the King of Italy, Victor Emanuel III. Being so short, he wouldn't normally have had to do military service. However, the statutory minimum height for joining the army was lowered that year, otherwise not even the future king of Italy would have been able to join the army. That's why my grandfather had to do military service.

He was a builder and, like him, all his sons had to work as builders, with the exception of my father, for he used to go around playing the guitar and harmonica at village festivals. My grandfather was builder to many rich families, including the family of the occupier of cities of whom I've spoken.

At home and at work he was as despotic as a king. When his sons had to do military service, he wanted them all to become carabinieri, even though the period of service was longer — that way they earned money and didn't waste time.

For him and his sons alike, holidays didn't count, and they worked Sundays like any other day. Not even religion counted as far as they were concerned, except for essentials such as baptisms, marriages and funerals. Not only did my grandfather not read papers, he even thought that the news reported in the papers was without foundation, and regarded news as stories that had been dreamt up and simply served to waste time.

One of the builder's sons soon had a row with my despotic grandfather, and went his own way and worked abroad. He stayed in France for several years, and used to say that in all those years he never noticed they talked French over there.

My grandfather and his sons used to talk in the dialect of their village, but just a mile or two from their home and the minute you crossed the Po, the dialects were quite different. When my uncle left home and started working near Genoa, he found a dialect very different from his own. And similarly he found very different dialects in all the places he stayed — Menton, Nice, Dijon. However, he always managed to make himself understood, and so as far as he was concerned, one dialect was like another.

Indeed, as my uncle used to say, what difference did it make whether he was talking to a Frenchman or a peasant on the Italian side of the border? He understood one a little and the other a little, but he could make himself understood with both of them.

Then his son was born. Two years later, he went back to work in Italy, leaving his wife in Dijon.

And it was only when he went back to France after a further two years, and listened to his son and discovered he spoke very differently from himself, that is, in a foreign language, that he pictured in his mind a fog-bound sea that it was impossible to cross: Over there, there's someone who is talking to you and you hear him, but you'll never manage to make yourself understood, because your mouth simply can't say things the way they are, and it'll always be an endless misunderstanding, one wrong word after another, a fog, like being at sea, while all the time others understand one another perfectly and are happy.

That's how my uncle discovered the existence of foreign languages, the first of the family to do so.

Hearing his son speaking in French — a son so small and yet already worlds away from the dialect of my despotic grandfather — was the biggest surprise of his life. It was as if he had awoken from a dream, and he started to cry.

The traveller's return

I set off by train for Polesella at dawn on a journey in search of the village where my mother was born, without knowing exactly where I was going. I had only a rough idea of where the village was, and hadn't found it on any road maps. I was counting on picking up a larger-scale map on the way so as to be able to locate it.

Before getting off the train at Ferrara, I'd seen a fellow half-asleep on his feet who wearily lifted his eyelids each time someone entered the station. Then, the eyelids fell shut and his head slumped forward with a slight jolt. Later, on getting off the train at Polesella, I found myself surrounded by people looking similarly shaky. People who, like me, had got up first thing in the morning with the feeling of not knowing where they were, who had left home semi-conscious of bodies which moved almost of their own volition, and now found themselves out there, ready to go anywhere. Some men in the station-bar were getting going by lighting their first cigarette.

When I asked where the centre of Polesella was, some boys sitting on chairs outside a bar replied scornfully that this was the centre. These boys had long hair and denim jackets. As they smoked, they laughed, were loud and noisy, and ate popcorn, all at eight in the morning.

The centre of the town consisted of two avenues divided by a flower bed with no plants. On either side of the street there were low houses with uniform and unadorned façades dating from the post-war period. And here it still seemed to be post-war — post a disaster of which nobody had heard a word. The entire length of the street was given over to the essentials of life — there was an electrical goods shop, a tobacconist's, a commercial agency, a chemist's, a women's hat-shop, and, at the far end of the avenue, a grey box with no roof that was the cinema, which was simply called CINEMA. It was showing a porno film.

Later on, I was in another part of the town trying to find maps. There was an empty merry-go-round, dodgem cars under plastic sheets, and the whole area was covered in tarmac, as if human beings should forget forever what the earth's surface is like.

From Polesella, I took a coach to Guarda Veneta, and during the journey I was frightened of speaking and hearing my own voice, like when I was in another continent. I avoided looking at other passengers so that they wouldn't turn and talk to me.

After Crespino and Villanova, further roadsigns read: CORBOLA / PAPOZZE. Fields with hardly any grass and here grey-coloured sheep were grazing right up to the edge of the canal. Beyond the canal, there were old houses with outside chimneys of the kind that narrow at first floor level and have chimney-stacks shaped like turrets that point up into the sky.

Lorry after lorry passed. It was raining, and with the dark sky it was difficult to make anything out. The coach had stopped in front of a long farm-building, crumbling and overgrown with ivy, even over the shutters. And, at the door, a woman emerged holding a basin in which she was rinsing her hair. The moment the woman saw that I was looking at her, she stiffened her neck, keeping it bent over the bowl. I'd have liked to have got out and talked to her, to learn what sort of words people might use in a place like that. Soon afterwards, a roadsign at a bend announced Adria.

Early in the afternoon in Adria, I went into a bar covered with posters about Football Pools prize money, in which a television towered over the small space and acted as a background to the men standing at the counter talking in dialect. The men were discussing an incident involving some person or other, and were debating whether it was best to go around armed. Someone suggested it was dangerous because 'that sort never look you in the eye.' I couldn't make out what they were saying. In front of the bar, a line of boys sheltering from the rain sat watching the tarmac, and along the road no cars passed. As I left, for one long moment you could hear only the noise of the Western on the television.

I found a hotel, a two-storey building with bare walls painted deep red and the sign ALBERGO LAGUNA. I was looking for maps in a stationery shop and a tired-looking young woman spoke to me very slowly, as if she were pondering every sentence she had to utter. She said: 'There's not a lot here', and then: 'Adria is out-of-the-way', and then: 'As you'll have seen for yourself.'

In this town, there were two or three main streets full of modern shops, bars, mopeds, and secluded streets where I found lovely old villas. Turning around, I saw a huge television-transmitter mast which seemed taller than any building in the town. In another shop, nobody had heard of the places where I had to go. It seemed they had been wiped forever from people's minds and from the maps.

Back at the hotel, I began reading a novel by Malcolm Lowry. After dinner, I watched television — a film with Stewart Granger and Deborah Kerr.

Leaving Adria, empty spaces open out in all directions as far as the eye can see. A motorway rounds a corner on a hill and joins another motorway with four lanes. That morning, it was full of lorries and cars that were racing along in the rain. From the top of this road, I could see the plains with grey fields dissected by canals, and a number of those lovely houses with turret-shaped chimneys — houses abandoned and crumbling, the roofs in pieces and the doors and windows bricked up.

From the moment I'd left Adria, I'd done nothing but follow the canals, into whose still waters the rain was falling. All around were farmhouses, fields of wheat, people bicycling along tracks, and small iron bridges where the occasional person under an umbrella was fishing.

As I was about to cross the Po, the land behind me dipped down into a hollow that stretched as far as the horizon. On a roadsign was a map showing the two banks of the river; I read the place names: TAGLIO DI PO / PORTO TOLLE.

The appearance of the passengers on the coach, along with the dirge-like sound of their voices, belonged to people who had long given up all nonsense, pretensions and unnecessary chatter. As the road was full of pot-holes, the coach squeaked continuously.

All of a sudden, without knowing why, I got off the coach; as luck would have it, the rain had stopped falling. The landscape either side of the long, straight road to Taglio di Po was dotted with electricity pylons that drew the eye unremittingly onward.

The low, distant horizon, half-hidden by what appeared to be a halo of rain, was broken by cypress trees and willows. The ditches were overrun by red rumex. In the fields were abandoned, roofless houses scattered here and there, whereas along the road were modern houses. All around, the fields of wheat were yellow and brooding; the maize still green.

When it began to rain across the length and breadth of the countryside, there was not a living soul to be seen. A driver, cornered while stopping in a small square, hesitated for some time before giving me a lift. He gave me long, searching looks. There was a photo of a child on the dashboard, and a patchwork puppy suspended from the mirror jerked up and down endlessly.

I didn't exchange a single word with the driver. Getting out of the car, what had looked like a fortress turned out to be a long line of postwar houses, along with clothes-, sports-, electrical-goods shops, and a number of bars. On the other side, the village looked out onto waste land and ruins as far as a point in the distance where I could see only mud and rocks. It was like being in some far-flung outpost. Dogs were poking around in a pile of rubbish.

The minute I tried to cross the road, all the drivers sounded their horns full blast. I was convinced that the drivers weren't going anywhere but just drove around ad infinitum at the slightest excuse, terrified of standing still. I watched them waiting impatiently in the rain at some traffic-lights, blowing their horns, desperate not to be standing still.

This village is called Taglio di Po, because men at one time had to split the river in two in order to direct its flow. Yet, climbing up the embankment to get a better view, I couldn't imagine that there had ever existed anything different from the space of our own time — the only one I had been given the opportunity of knowing. And all I could find on the embankment was a sign saying: NOMADS AND TRAVELLERS — NO STOPPING. Further on, there was a field full of scattered rubbish, including empty cans, the shreds of an old suitcase, part of a heater. Under the embankment were the squat houses of ex-fishermen, a landscape dotted with grey industrial sheds and no one to be seen.

The bridge over the Po, under which I'd taken cover, was a cement casting set on eight or ten pillars. Underneath ran the blue tubes of a huge gas pipeline. The rain was beating down, and some birds were gliding over the river banks, almost touching the ground.

In the middle of the afternoon, I was crossing the bridge in the direction of Piano, taking roads that were broad and straight, and slightly undulating. The dark sky with its low horizons seemed endless, and lorries that passed lifted wings of spray from the sides of the road. Then, when I asked directions under the shelter of a service station, a pump attendant gesticulated impatiently, as if he was sick of the sight of other people's faces.

I left the roads with their heavy traffic, heading for the banks of the Po Grande along tracks that passed by houses with orchards surrounded by cane fencing. In one house, there was a man who was watching television with his hat on. At a certain point, the man called out a woman's name, then turned to look out of the window, but did not see me. Two May bugs and a column of ants were dispersing in the gravel amid lumps of brick and plaster.

It was about six o'clock in the evening and the sky was growing darker when I set off along a wide road, not knowing where it would lead. A signpost informed me that the 45th parallel passed through that very point. I was mid-way between the North Pole and the Equator.

Walking with my hood up, I couldn't see anything either side of me. I didn't manage to flag down any cars. They all drove on into the mist that had now fallen.

The next morning in Goro — I'd got a lift that night — I was given details about where I had to go. I was told I had got the route completely wrong. The train on the old local line from Bologna to Portomaggiore took just three hours, while it was an hour by car from Ferrara.

It was Sunday. The weather had cleared and drivers were more willing to give lifts. I got a lift as far as Ostellato, then another towards Portomaggiore.

At a crossroads, one driver said to me as I was getting out of his car: 'It's time for the beast to go and eat.' I thought he meant me, and yet he was talking about himself.

At Dogato, I asked a man who was out walking his dog if he knew the village I was looking for. The man was happy to talk, but couldn't tell me anything about any of the places. So he walked with me for a while, talking about this and that. Then, later on, he invited me for a meal in a bar where they also sold newspapers and had a whole shelf full of pornographic magazines. We talked about the weather and the fact that, a few centuries earlier, the place had been on the sea and Portomaggiore had been a large port.

The land, by now, was very rich, with orchards everywhere. The uniformly flat horizon was no longer barren and threatening, as on the previous day. In the distance, the orchards in blossom looked just like copses, forming rose-coloured shapes that stood out against the background landscape.

Coming from Ostellato, the whole length of the winding road is bordered by plane trees. I saw acacias, too, in the surrounding area and numerous canals where fishermen made me think once more of my people and their way of life. In a field, a flock of seagulls were circling around something, and I could hear their cries.

I walked along this road as far as another crossroads. To the left, there was a narrow road and a small roadsign on the ground which said: SANDOLO. This is the village where my mother was born.

I sat on a milestone and tried to picture it to myself. In the background, I could see the squat bell-tower of a church, its metal point glistening in the sun. At one time this place must have consisted of a few fields under cultivation, a lot of marshland, and nothing much else — everything flat and deserted. When my mother left this village she must have been seven or eight years old.

I tried to conjure up an image of something, but I just saw vague pictures of haystacks, old-fashioned carriages and cobbled roads. I had a vision of a tiny church with a terracotta facade.

The other side of the crossroads, I couldn't see anything — just empty countryside and that squat bell-tower. I could imagine nothing of other times and other situations. Out of a house on the road, a girl emerged who leaned forward to see what I was doing sitting there on the milestone. Then I turned back towards Ostellato.

Out in the open

Just before the last world war, there arrived in the country district around Portomaggiore, in the province of Ferrara, a man who used to go about the countryside selling material, needles and thread. He also sold clothes patterns, which could be seen in finished form in a catalogue, and people would buy cut-outs of these separately to place over the material, thereby guaranteeing a cut that matched the style of the pattern and the model in every detail. The man drove around in a Balilla car and wore a Borsalino hat pulled down over his eyes. He was always smiling and had a fine line in sales talk. He used to sleep in the car or in a barn, eat in his clients' homes (knocking the cost of the meal off the price of any goods purchased), and accept payment in flour, beans and maize.

At that time, there weren't any bars in the country districts. So, to while away the evenings, the man would get a tenant farmer and his family to gather round and he told them stories.

One evening, before making for the barn to sleep, the man caressed a young girl who was looking at him wide-eyed, evidently greatly impressed by his stories. That night, two men entered the barn and savagely beat the travelling salesman, who only just managed to jump into his car and make his escape into the surrounding countryside. Then no more was heard of him.

One day, about twenty years later, a one-eyed man arrived in the vicinity. He asked a lot of questions around the place.

Finally, he said he'd lost his eye right there, in front of the farm building where he was standing, twenty years earlier. Two men had attacked him during the night, accusing him of being a pervert, and had hit him in the eye as he was running out of the barn.

A woman standing on the doorstep of the farmhose, who had been observing him for some time and listening to his story, said she remembered everything. She was the child the man had caressed that evening, and she remembered his stories and the evenings around the kitchen table. She had got married to a tenant farmer a lot older than herself who had beaten and maltreated her for several years, and had then died, suffocated by haemoptysis. He was probably the very same tenant farmer that had hit the travelling salesman with a shovel, causing the loss of an eye.

During the course of the conversation, the woman did nothing to conceal the hatred she still felt for her late husband and his brutal ways, nor did she hide her liking for the unfortunate ex-travelling salesman. She invited him into her kitchen for a drink and spoke freely with him.

She said that men in that part of the world would never show their feelings and caress a young girl they didn't know. They always had to appear tough and give everyone surly looks, so as not to be caught out by other men.

When taking his leave on the doorstep, the one-eyed man confessed to the woman that he had just come out of prison where he'd spent eighteen years. He had strangled a young girl.

He immediately added that all his ideas and feelings, moods and inclinations had changed utterly during his years in prison. He was now happy to have settled his account with the law, because this had made him used to the idea of being out in the open, whatever the time or place.

The woman on the doorstep had not moved, but she no longer looked the man in the face as she had done. Now she was looking at the ground. Then, the one-eyed man headed towards the car parked in the threshing yard, and, on reaching the car, turned to speak to her. He told her that everything looks different when you feel yourself to be out in the open, when you stop believing you can hide somewhere and be safe.

The life of an unknown storyteller

There was, at that time, a desert along that stretch of the Libyan coast. Going inland from the sea, shelves of rock rose up in steps. A deep cave had been dug under the first rock-shelf. On the morning of 21 January 1941, a group of officers and soldiers woke up to the sound of guns firing and a voice outside the cave saying in English: 'Come on out!'

The two senior officers immediately cocked their pistols to show they had every intention of committing suicide.

However, one of the two men then asked a lieutenant with a squint: 'What shall we do?' The squint-eyed lieutenant suggested: 'Let's surrender.' 'Very well,' replied the senior officer, 'See to it.'

The squint-eyed lieutenant pushed three rifles out of the cave, and a black hand that seemed to him enormous grabbed them. All the while the voice kept saying: 'Come on out!'

The group of officers and soldiers left the cave with their hands up. The squint-eyed lieutenant left along with the others and was herded into a line. While they were waiting to be herded across the desert, he began writing his first novel. He noted down the opening words on the back of a postcard: 'I've been a prisoner-of-war for ten minutes. Just one step and everything has changed.'

About a year and a half later, he was in the Yol prison-camp at the foot of the Himalayas. This camp of wooden huts provided accommodation for ten thousand officers, many of whom were accompanied by their orderlies, who continued to serve them, polish their boots and do their laundry. The life of officer-prisoners in the Yol camp was that of a mass of tourists faced with the inevitable question of how to pass the time.

They used to do PT, learn English and play tennis. In the afternoons, they were free to go for walks outside the camp in the direction of the sacred grove called the Wood of Monkeys. Some of them put on plays, others organized exhibitions of paintings. A library furnished with English and Italian books made it possible for them to do a good deal of reading. The frequent love affairs between men were sometimes kept hidden, sometimes openly mocked by everyone else. Indian boys from outside the camp used to offer themselves to the Italian officers for a couple of rupees.

The squint-eyed lieutenant asked the camp authorities to be sent to Europe to fight the Nazis. His request was turned down, so he then learnt to be docile, quiescent and unsociable, and just consider himself as a tourist-prisoner. He finished writing his first novel, and then wrote some plays which were put on at the camp theatre.

For forty years he continued to write every day, and contiues even now. He now spends every morning writing in a patisserie shop in Ravenna in which he feels at home, mainly, in my opinion, because not once in ten years has he exchanged a word with anyone. For forty years his novels have been regularly refused by whichever publisher or whichever man of letters he has approached. Nothing he has written day in, day out for forty years has ever been published.

The stories that he tells are sedate, sentimental and polite, written in a language no one would know how to write in any longer, and in a tone no one will ever use again. (He reads Montaigne every day.)

He is now seventy years old. He's tall, very good-looking and has a squint. He is so unused to speaking that, when he phones me and decides to utter a few words, the sound that issues from his throat is that of an animal waking up. His wife, on the other hand, is always making jokes in dialect, and when she makes jokes, he laughs silently to himself. They never had children, and live in a small flat on the eighth floor of an apartment block.

The perpetual motion machine type II

A German friend told me the story of a worker from the Ruhr who had designed and was trying to build the perpetual motion machine type II.

Perpetual motion of type I is supposed to be generated by a machine which, without consuming energy, can produce an unlimited motion and hence an unlimited source of mechanical energy. Perpetual motion of type II, on the other hand, is supposed to be generated by a machine able to transform heat into mechanical energy, and then reconvert the mechanical energy into heat, and the heat back again into mechanical energy and so on, without any leakage and so without needing anything else to keep going.

In 1949, the worker Rudiger Fiess, wrote a letter to the Federal Chancellor, Adenauer, explaining the thing to him and sending him his design. Adenauer replied with a letter in his own handwriting in which he acknowledged Fiess's discovery of perpetual motion, and promised that he would personally see to obtaining funding and thereby make it possible for him to build his projected machine.

During the next decade, Fiess waited in vain for the funding to arrive. He sent numerous letters requesting it without ever receiving a reply. In 1954, the house where he was living burnt down, and his design and all his calculations were lost, together with Chancellor Adenauer's letter.

I don't know what Fiess did in the intervening period and whether he carried on studying the problem of perpetual motion. The fact is, around the mid-sixties, a serious accident forced him to give up his job as a crane-operator, and this enabled him to devote all his time to the project he'd had in mind for years.

As he paused for a moment opposite a factory that was being demolished on the building site where he was working, the ball of a crane swung by, smashing his hip and thigh-bone. Fiess would remain a cripple for the rest of his life.

An insurance company paid him a large sum in compensation and he decided, as he was married to an Italian woman, to move to Italy, to the place his wife came from, that is near Porto Garibaldi, in the province of Ravenna. Here he rented an old, disused hangar not far from his house, and began, in that hangar, single-handedly to build the machine of his dreams.

When, in 1978, my friend Reinhard Dellit, came to Porto Garibaldi to make a documentary about Fiess's machine, which he'd heard a lot about, Fiess wouldn't let him into the hangar for a number of days. First he wanted to ascertain Reinhard's intentions and the purpose of the documentary; then, to be sure that Reinhard really was in a position to grasp the fundamentals of his project.

What my friend saw and filmed in the hangar is rather difficult to describe.

At the centre of the hangar, there were four large iron wheels which formed a square, and these turned on axles, from which a system of cams and ball-bearings ensured that their motion was interconnected and synchronic. That, according to Fiess, was the heart of the machine.

From the heart of the machine, pivoting arms branched upwards, connecting with smaller wheels of varying sizes before forming an architectural structure made of wheels and worm-wheels and pivoting arms that extended haphazardly into space.

At fixed points along the aerial joints, there were trip-mechanisms with connecting rods and hammer-shaped counterweights at the bottom. When the machine was in motion, these hammers plummeted onto plates fixed at regular intervals on the rim of the smaller wheels or the four large wheels. The hammer gave the plate a great blow, setting that wheel and the connecting wheels into motion, then returning, thanks to the trip-mechanism, ready to deliver another blow in due course.

In fact, the pivoting joints were synchronized with the smaller and larger wheels on the basis of calculations regarding the weight of the hammer and the length of the arm and the trip-mechanism, in order to come a semi-circle and, in due course, use up the inertial push at the topmost point from which the hammers then fell once more, delivering further blows or kicks to the wheel-plates, depending on the type of motion required at that point — whether from the top down or the bottom up.

From what my German friend had given me to understand, Fiess continued for a while to add wheels and pivoting joints in different directions, and re-doing the calculations in order to synchronize their motion with the motion of the existing wheels and joints.

Soon after that, he added some trip mechanisms to the machine at the far end of the hangar, attaching them to a series of big rubber balls with handles — the ones children use for sitting on and jumping up and down like frogs. And this (an exercise in the exploitation of the bounce in particularly elastic bodies) was the final attempt at obtaining a continuous and co-ordinated movement of the whole apparatus.

The problem Fiess expounded to Reinhard — i.e. his basic idea — consisted in this: obtaining a perpetual motion type II not by transforming heat into mechanical energy, but by using the force of gravity and inertia alone.

However, Fiess also explained that all the calculations in the project sent to Chancellor Adenauer in 1949 had been exact, because he had had them checked by an engineer he knew, and the original machine had been much simpler (it seems he had made a wooden model). Yet that design had been lost in the fire in his house, and he now didn't recall precisely how he had solved certain problems.

At that time, that is in 1978, the machine, when set in motion by pushing one of the wheels, managed to keep moving for about fifty seconds. According to Reinhard, the man no longer had hopes of obtaining a perpetual motion proper, but was spellbound by that vast synchronic movement of wheels, pivoting joints, trip-mechanisms, connecting-rods, hammers and rubber balls.

He used to spend the whole day in the hangar watching the wheels move.

According to Fiess, the world was going wrong because God had abandoned it to its fate at the hands of red terrorists and Asians. In Germany, for example, there are too many Turks everywhere — Turks with hideous faces, he says — who go dancing on Sundays, as if it were the most natural thing in the world.

The story of the woman racing-cyclist and her suitor

The ranks of the competitors in the 1924 Tour of Italy were decimated by the toughest of routes, and only thirty out of the ninety starters managed to make it to the end of the race, after having pedalled along dusty roads for more than 3,500 kilometres. At the finishing line, the crowd applauded the winner, but reserved an even warmer reception for the last cyclist home. This cyclist had reached Milan despite a series of bad falls, despite being excluded from the race on a mountain stage for exceeding the qualifying time, despite not having backing, apart from the two meals a day paid for by the tyre company whose name was on her jersey, and, finally, despite the fact that she was a woman.

The papers dubbed her *la corridora.* She was a short, stocky girl, came from a peasant family, and was the only woman in the history of cycle racing to get to compete in official races alongside the so-called 'champions of the pedal', who, as a rule, are men.

A photo of the period shows her bent over the handlebars of a racing bike, large shorts down to her knees, speeding along a country lane to the applause of a row of supporters, who are all barefoot. She has a round face with large occipital bones, a very broad forehead and small eyes, and her hair is swept back. She has big calves, burly arms, square shoulders. She has a smile the shape of a half-moon whose corners are lost in her bulging cheeks.

This photo is hung in the shop of a cobbler from Ariano Polesine who for years suffered a hellish torment from being madly in love with that woman cyclist.

Emigrating to Milan with his father at the age of twelve, he had taken courses in fashion design, studying in the evenings, and had won first prize in a national competition for designers of women's footwear. He didn't take much interest in sport, but, reading the papers, he developed a passionate interest in the exploits of the woman racing-cyclist. And, one evening, in the wake of that particularly demanding Tour of Italy, he managed to get himself invited to a banquet in her honour, and finally to meet her.

The woman cyclist had married a silversmith. He had whisked her away, at the age of fifteen, from a family in which the parents could not come to terms with the idea that a woman should devote herself to a man's sport, and he had given her the freedom to pursue a career as a racing-cyclist.

The night of the banquet, the designer, after looking at her for an hour, had fallen in love and immediately gone and made known his feelings. The woman cyclist could not accept his declaration of love as she was happily married to the silversmith, and so turned him down point-blank.

The next day, the designer sent her a presentation pair of the women's shoes he had designed and styled, but the racing-cyclist sent them back with the message: 'I'm only interested in bicycles.'

In the light of the international acclaim she won in the Tour of Italy, the woman cyclist was asked to race in Paris. Here she raced for some time on the tracks, invariably competing against male cyclists, and it is to this city that she returned when her husband died.

The designer, who had gained a commendation in an international exhibition of women's shoes held in Paris during the same period, shot off to the French capital to ask the woman cyclist to marry him. After many fruitless attempts to get in touch with her, he wrote her a letter and sent her a presentation pair of the shoes for which he had gained such coveted recognition at the Paris exhibition.

He withdrew to his hotel for the evening to await her reply. The reply arrived straightaway, together with the return of a solitary shoe (it's not known what happened to the other) and the usual message: 'I'm only interested in bicycles.'

That evening, the designer, all alone in his hotel room and overcome by despair, boiled the patent-leather shoe that had been returned to him and ate it piece by piece.

The woman cyclist remarried almost immediately — this time to a racing-cyclist who was the world number one in the 500-metre sprint — and she and he appeared together for a while on the French tracks. She went back to Italy and, with her husband, opened a tyre shop in Milan.

When her second husband also died, she kept the business going by herself, as a way of staying in touch with the cycling world, repairing tyres and following the races of her protégés.

One day, the designer turned up again — except by this time he was no longer a designer, because he had given up this vocation in the meantime, and had gone all round Europe on foot, as far as Belgium and Holland, repairing shoes in country districts, and eventually getting arrested for being a tramp.

Once again, the ex-designer, now a mere mender of shoes, asked the ex-cyclist to marry him. Once again, she turned him down, treating him very badly because he was more interested in shoes than bicycles. She could not accept such a husband.

Even though she had retired from racing years earlier, the ex-cyclist still enjoyed a certain popularity in the world of cycling, which she had no intention of leaving until the day she died. She followed all her protégés' races on a large motorcycle, and carried on doing so, riding her large motorcycle until the day she died, at the age of sixty-eight.

The ex-designer, now a mere cobbler in a small town in Polesine, went to her funeral.

One evening before the end of the world

I have heard a story told about a woman who used to work as a secretary for a transport company near Taglio di Po. She was a beautiful woman with large breasts who always wore black stockings and tight-fitting clothes. Ever since her husband died and her son moved to Venezuela to work in a restaurant near a magnesium mine, the woman had lived by herself.

She made friends with a middle-aged teacher who worked in Contarina and also lived by herself. The two women started seeing each other every day and having dinner together every evening, as well as sleeping together on frequent occasions.

Then the teacher was left shaken by news of an impending catastrophe, after she had read something about the build-up of anhydrous carbons in the atmosphere due to the fumes discharged by the world's cities.

She explained to her friend that a big build-up of anhydrous carbons in the atmosphere, similar to the one taking place, would cause a disasterous rise in temperature on the planet leading to the melting of the polar ice-cap and the submersion of whole continents. She went on to explain that the only parts safe from the catastrophe, at least in the short term, were the higher points close to the pole, like the Norwegian mountains. This was because there would be less heat and less danger of submersion there because of the altitude.

The two women must have discussed these things at some

length, and convinced themselves that the catastrophe was imminent — a matter of months.

They therefore decided, one fine day, to go and spend their summer holidays in Norway, thinking that, should anything happen over the summer, they would be in a safe place.

They left in August and stayed in Norway until mid-September. Then, seeing that nothing had happened, they returned home and went back to work.

The following summer they went back to the same mountains for another holiday, always more or less ready for the catastrophe. During the holidays one of the two women — the teacher — got to know an extremely rich man from Switzerland, who had also moved there. The two decided to marry, and the teacher returned to Italy to put her things in order. Then she came straight back to get married to the Swiss man.

So, in early August the woman from Taglio di Po found herself alone once more. She was reckoning on taking retirement at the earliest opportunity and also moving to Norway for good, thereby rejoining the only friend she had.

She would have had to wait three years to qualify for retirement, but she felt lonely and decided to change her way of life.

She found a job in a shipping office in Sottomarina near Chioggia, and went to live in a small flat on the outskirts of Chioggia. She became a vegetarian and bought a machine for making juices out of tomatoes, carrots, melons and citrus fruit. She used to get through a lot of vegetables, lentils, beans, chick-peas, brown rice, and soya. At work she ate biscuits made from corn flour.

She enrolled for an evening class in yoga run by a couple of ex-students in an old Venetian house in Chioggia. She also began attending an evening class in English, and read books about diet, books about natural treatments for circulatory illnesses, and a book about the pollution of the atmosphere.

She started having an affair with one of the two students who took the yoga classes, and became a devotee of the baroque music her lover liked so much. When the yoga course finished and her lover disappeared from the scene without saying a word, she started going for evening walks with a mineral water supplier, who was married with three children.

This brings us to the June of a year or so ago — the month the woman took her own life.

It is necessay to say that her meetings with the mineral water supplier were often alluded to in the shipping office where she worked, taking the form of repeated jokes about mineral water. For his part, the supplier, after (unsuccessful) attempts to persuade her to abandon the idea of going to Norway and to stop thinking about atmospheric catastrophe, cut down on his evening visits. Eventually he too disappeared without saying a thing.

However, the yoga teacher had reappeared again. The woman often went looking for him, but he made it clear that, as far as their relationship was concerned, he didn't want to know.

One evening in June, as the office was about to lock up, the woman walked into a conversation between two clerks who were talking between sniggers about the good fortune enjoyed by suppliers of mineral water, and about the 'godsend' that one of them had got his hands on. Whereupon, the woman began to unbutton her top and loosen her dress, challenging them with the words: 'Do you want to have a go too?'. She was in the middle of stripping when she was immobilized, forcibly dressed and taken outside.

That evening, instead of going straight home, she took a stroll in the main square in Chioggia. She went up to the dock to look at the sea, and then stopped by a Venetian column which some boys on scooters were riding up and down in front of. About eight o'clock the thoroughfare emptied, leaving mostly tourists and young people in boaters at the open-air cafés under the arcades.

In one of these cafés the yoga teacher was busy discussing football. The woman went and talked to him, saying she felt lonely and that she loved him. The yoga teacher replied quite frankly that she had a depressing effect on him, because being near someone who was always thinking about global catastrophe was depressing. The woman turned her back on him and left.

She walked as far as the harbour packed with fishing-boats — cars and mopeds along the canal, people sitting outside their front doors in the cool of the evening, and young lads swarming around the videogames arcade. Here, around nine o'clock, someone who knew her called out to her, but she didn't reply.

Once home, she sealed the doors and windows with wet towels, turned on the gas in the kitchen and put on a record of baroque music. Two acquaintances of hers — a married couple — were passing by; when they heard the music and saw lights in the groundfloor windows, they rang the door-bell. But the woman inside didn't answer. She was busy watering the indoor plants and putting nylon covers over them.

As her two acquaintances began knocking, the woman sat on the floor, wrapped her head in a white jumper and her entire body in a length of nylon of the kind used in shipping goods. Then, wrapped in this manner, she lay down on the floor.

It was still a bright, clear evening, with just an occasional cloud on the horizon. An hour before, the sky had clouded over, but then a current of air had blown from the east, and shreds of cloud were now scudding above the long bridge that crossed the lagoon. Her two acquaintances had gone about a hundred yards and were about to get into their car and go to Chioggia for an ice cream when there was a big explosion in the woman's house.

The woman was dead on arrival at the hospital. Why she had wrapped herself up like that — like a parcel — and why she had taped up her mouth, and her eyes and nose, even her sexual organs, no one could say.

How a photographer landed in the New World

Ca' Venier is not so much a proper village as an area of houses scattered along the main part of the river, the Po di Venezia, before it divides into its two main branches — the Po di Pila and the Po di Gnocca — on its journey towards the inlets of the lagoon and then on to the sea. Wherever one is in this area there is little to be seen in any direction except stretches of cultivated fields, mostly of wheat. Further on towards Ca' Zullian, marshlands loom on the horizon, but everywhere the eye can see there are straight roads crossing the flat, unchanging terrain that used to be lagoons before they were filled in.

Nothing could be less promising from a photographic point of view than this landscape, whose flatness and uniformity extend as far as the fringes of land that jut out into the sea. And out to sea little islands pop up here and there, like so many tongues of sand. Some emerge only at low tide, while others, fringed by grasses that hold back the mud carried seaward by the big river, are home to clumps of reeds visible from far off and other plants suited to the salt-water environment — this is called the foreshore.

One day a photographer was sent by a popular weekly magazine to take photographs of this area. His photos had to illustrate a text that a famous writer was to write on 'the humble folk of the mouth of the Po'.

After he'd taken photographs of the river channels at sunset, of a few heavily-clad women gathering grasses by the roadside a few old women bent double carrying canes on their backs, the seagulls above a lagoon plus a boat on the water, the photographer had run out of ideas and was about to go home. It was just then that he heard that the women in these parts went to the cemetery to talk to the dead, holding actual conversations with deceased members of their family beside their gravestones. He therefore decided to take some pictures of a few women absorbed in conversation with the dead. Staking out a position in the cemetery of Ca' Venier one afternoon, he secretly took a few shots with a powerful telephoto lens. He then sent the negatives to his magazine and went off to Venice for the weekend.

There wasn't much to be seen in the photos taken in the Ca' Venier cemetery except a woman dressed in black who,with her lips parted, was making a gesture in front of a gravestone. The editors of the magazine asked the photographer to go back to the area, make contact with someone, get them to explain exactly what the dead were saying, and perhaps take a few photos with more dramatic poses. This was so that the readers would get a clearer idea of what went on in these cemeteries.

And so, returning to the area, the photographer came upon a different cemetery, and here he tried to approach a woman dressed in black who was kneeling in front of a grave, and interview her using a miniature microphone built into a button of his jacket. However, not only did this woman not reply, she didn't even look up at his face but left the place straightaway along with the other women who had been there among the graves. Finding himself alone and not knowing what to do, the photographer noticed he was being watched from a distance by an extremely thin man. This, as he quickly learnt, was the caretaker of the cemetery.

Unlike the women-folk of the village, the thin man stopped to talk to him. He informed him that the dead there confided only in the women, and, after he'd smoked a cigarette offered him by the photographer, he told him his whole life story and invited him to his house.

He was born on one of those lagoons that are now filled in, and for many years had been a gamekeeper living in a thatched hut, where people out shooting coots would come and ask him to guide them through the valleys and marshes. He had then been bought by an oil man from Ravenna who kept a boat at the mouth of the Po, which he had to look after over the winter months, and on which he served as sailor and fisherman when the oil man wanted to go out to sea. When he had sold the boat, the oil man also sold the thin man, together with all the fishing equipment, to people who never used to come to the area. Consequently the man still did the job of looking after the boat, but could also do other things like go fishing in his own boat and mind the cemetery.

The man's face was all furrowed and wrinkled. On his head he wore a kind of fur hat and under his jacket a cowboy-style checked shirt.

Not until they were sitting at the table in the man's home — a house comprising a single room furnished with shiny new furniture — did the photographer notice that three fingers were missing from the old fisherman's right hand. After he had told him his life story, the thin man wanted also to tell him how he'd lost the fingers that were missing.

Right after the war he'd spent some time around Chioggia, where there were lots of German bunkers and where cartridges and hand-grenades could be found all over the place. The children used to empty the cartridges and hand-grenades and light the gunpowder for fun. This is how the man lost his fingers — he was trying to help a child put a hand-grenade back together to preserve a bit of powder when he set off the percussion cap, and then saw one finger flying into the air, another dangling from his hand, and a thumb no longer there.

The thin man, still speaking mostly in dialect, confided to the photographer that he occasionally felt pain in his hand just where there had once been an index finger (he pointed to the empty spot with the other index finger) — pain like an attack of arthritis or else pins-and-needles.

The missing index finger had a current going through it. He knew exactly how a compass needle worked because the current passing through his index finger always pointed somewhere just like a compass. This ability of his index finger to point in a certain direction had helped him find a number of things he had lost, because sometimes if he was looking for something or other his index finger would begin 'pointing'.

The man said that his missing finger had even played a trick on him on one occasion. It had pointed out all the right scores in the football matches, and he'd written them down on a pools coupon and was on the way to becoming a millionaire. However he'd then lost the coupon before he had handed it in, and the finger didn't help him find it again until the following Sunday, by which time he'd got the results from the television.

The thin man was talking in all seriousness. The photographer was listening, amused by his seriousness. However, as it was getting late by this time, he wanted to bring the conversation round to the cemetery and the dead who used to talk only to the women.

The fisherman confirmed that this was so. If, however, the photographer was curious to know what the dead said, perhaps asking his missing index finger about it could help.

He therefore held up his mutilated hand and began to hit at the empty space of his missing fingers with his other hand. Meanwhile he explained to the photographer that there were places on one or two islands, or on the sandbanks of the foreshore out to sea, where you could hear what the dead were saying. He had occasionally come across them when out hunting or fishing, but always by chance, and he had never managed to track them down afterwards.

If he could now manage to get some feeling back into his missing index finger by slapping it, perhaps it might point in a particular direction and they could then head that way the next day.

The photographer, amused by these explanations, let him talk until the time came to go to bed. Around midnight he went to sleep on a camp bed the fisherman had offered him.

Early in the morning the fisherman woke him saying his finger was 'pointing'. It was necessary to get a move on and go where the finger sent them.

They headed off in the photographer's car towards a spot on the other side of the village of Pila, where a channel between two marshy areas flows into the sea. Here they climbed into a boat that the thin man kept among the bog grass and began rowing towards the sea.

The rest of the journey became an increasingly strange adventure for the photographer. Rowing towards the sandbanks of the foreshore and distant islands, some of them full of birds that are rarely seen, the fisherman reeled off the fantastic names given to these islands out in the sea — Barea, Zoaglia, Ca' Morta, Morosina, Pegaso, Bacucca.

Until they were pointing towards a small dune on the water which was full of birds that flew off at their arrival and which his guide called Nuovo Mondo, the New World; and then the photographer realized they had reached their destination.

And here, after asking the photographer to disembark quickly and get on with listening to the dead, the fisherman turned the boat around, abandoning him amidst the mud and rushes on a few square yards of land, yet not without explaining — though already with his back to him and rowing further and further away — that the missing finger had taken him to Nuovo Mondo and the very same finger had ordered that he stay there.

How everything that exists began

There is a very old and toothless man who says he knows how everything that exists began. He first became aware of it one night when looking at the sky and he later studied it in books.

When I got to know this old man he had been in hospital for many months, wrapped in gauze and in a pair of grey cloth pyjamas given him by the nurses. In the big room where we used to eat, his place was in one corner, under a statuette of Christ with its own green illumination. The television was always on in the room and the nurses, when they were serving the food, always used to joke about how he was so old that women had lost interest in him and that was why he was at peace with the world. The old man just about managed a smile and raised his eyes to watch television.

After lunch we used to take a walk along the main avenue in the hospital grounds — he in his pyjamas with a hat on his head and hands behind his back. If another patient asked him to have a coffee in a bar on the avenue which was regularly used by doctors, nurses, medical students and visitors, he declined the invitation saying that it was best if the sick didn't mix with the healthy. He used to have a coffee from a drinks machine in a storeroom whose walls were covered in obscene graffiti.

In his opinion, it all began like this — there was a cloud of dust up there in the endless darkness. And when he says endless darkness he means that one can't imagine where the darkness used to end.

The darkness was extremely cold, and it was a cold that probably even froze stones. We can't imagine this cold either because we can't imagine how a stone could possibly freeze on the inside.

Through the darkness there came fierce winds from every quarter that apparently swept away anything and everything, and that too is unimaginable.

In the cold darkness all that existed was a big cloud of dust, perhaps suspended in one place. He does not know whether it has always been there.

However, in his opinion, it transpired that the wind, by blowing so hard from every quarter, drove the particles of dust into one another. And the particles, colliding with incredible force, got grazed and gave off sparks.

It is the same as when two stones are rubbed together, for stones are in fact compressed particles of dust.

It was from these sparks, in his opinion, that fire originated. But it must also have been the case that the dust particles compacted by the fierce winds formed big stones that were hurled into the endless darkness, only to collide and burst into flames on impact.

That, therefore, is how some small stars came into being.

Next, it is necessary to examine what fire does. Around a fire are gusts of heat that you can feel with your hands. The same thing happened up there; gusts of heat were given off that then produced evaporation due to the extreme cold, just like when window panes mist up.

The gusts of heat, because of the intense cold all around, formed a bladder. It is a bladder with a skin of ice, for heat that advances towards the cold is resistant, but if the cold is intense it freezes. Just look at the skin of ice that forms on window-panes in winter.

The universe is one big bladder driven here and there in the darkness by the fierce winds, but as we are down here we cannot be aware of it. Yet if the stars weren't in the bladder, they would go out because of the fierce winds.

When he looks at the stars at night, he sees they are shining and that means they are big stones on fire. Then if one looks at the way the whole sky goes round at night, one can see that nothing in this bladder ever stops moving.

He does not know why those big stones continue going round inside the bladder. They say that there is also the force of gravity pushing, but this he cannot say since he is no scientist.

One day the bladder will burst and everything will start all over again. It is even possible that the astronauts, by exploring other planets, may one day make a hole in the bladder and then it will all end with a bang.

Perhaps the fierce wind that has created everything is God. But it would not be God as he is taught in church, because it is impossible to imagine him.

God is probably a fierce wind coming from the endless darkness.

One day while walking along the avenues in the hospital complex, the old man saw some dust on the ground which was being swept up in eddies by the wind. He stopped to look at it and told me that this dust, like all the dust that exists, comes from the spaces between the stars and this is something no one ever gives any thought to.

On earth everyone is made of dust that comes down from the sky, and when one dies one's dust continues to exist but has to change its appearance. He knows that when he dies he will become a mosquito.

The old people and his father used to say that mosquitoes are the dead come back. Yet this was perhaps only in his part of the country where there used to be lots of mosquitoes, due to the swamps. They then reclaimed the land everywhere and drained the valleys of the delta, and now there are very few mosquitoes, and he doesn't know what will happen.

However, he has already said to his friends: 'When I die and you see a mosquito coming into the house, don't drive it away because it'll be me paying you a call.'

Young humans on the run

There used in the not so distant past to be a vast dance hall in the part of the plain south of the big river that is nearest the mountains, and it had a luminous sign over it which could be seen in the countryside for miles around. Every evening thousands of cars came over from a nearby tile-manufacturing town — a town of straight roads, factories, and big blocks of flats surrounded by wasteland — and filled up the enormous open space in front of the hall. At weekends, motorists came from every direction — from the three main towns in the vicinity, from the surrounding countryside, and from the remote villages in the low-lying areas of the river basin — and crowded into this place, which attracted more people than any other dance hall in the area.

Gangs were often sent by owners of other dance halls to wreck the place, to provoke violent fights, and thus get it closed down. Consequently, the owner of the vast dance hall had hired some policemen who were given the job of intervening the moment anyone picked a fight, made a threatening gesture or pulled out a knife.

The policemen would take him to some small room and, before kicking him out the back entrance, would beat him about the head with a truncheon for some time, so that he would lose all interest in coming back to the place again.

The policemen in the back room would beat a person up for

some time and in such a way as not to leave any marks. In fact, they had no right to make arrests, let alone beat people up, for they used to work at the dance hall when they were off duty to earn an extra salary. But then the owner of the hall also paid a salary to the policemen's superiors who were always ready, should the need arise, to make a statemement saying that their men were indeed on duty.

During one brawl, policemen armed with truncheons dragged a youth away and smashed in one of his temples. And when the youth's companions burst into the back room, all they found was their friend lying dead on a table.

The owner of the dance hall came along and said they'd have to run for it if they didn't want to be arrested, because the police were on their way. So the four of them ran out the back entrance carrying their dead friend with them.

They made their escape through the darkness heading in the direction of the tile-manufacturing town. As they were going around a bend, they noticed a police road-block ahead of them, and so made a last-minute turn down a track running through the fields as a policeman fired a burst from his machine-gun, riddling one of the engines with holes. The four abandoned the car that had been hit and drove away through the fields in the other car, with its lights switched off. They decided not to go home and face arrest.

They headed north towards the big river, getting lost in the grid of minor roads that go off in all directions. At dawn they found themselves under a menacing sky in an utterly deserted area, not far from a factory that makes nuclear shelters — a factory still in existence today and which they had heard about at the time. And when they came out onto a straight road used only by lorries, it was the large factory sign that gave them some indication as to where they were.

Under the large sign they met an Arab carpet-seller who was setting out his wares on the verge — carpets, clocks, lighters, knick-knacks. All around there were gloomy-looking huts whose doors and windows were shut. Nothing went by except lorries driven at high speed.

When talking to the Arab, the four youths learnt that, if you followed this road as far as the river, you came to a camp near a bridge which was full of homeless people from other countries — Jugoslavs, Africans, Gypsies and other foreigners living in makeshift huts inside a barbed-wire perimeter fence. They were foreigners with no passports who had come to the area in search of work, and had been put in this camp to await being shipped back home or settled somewhere else. They also learnt from the Arab that in practice anyone could get into the camp through the barbed-wire, and that no one ever came to check on who was living in the huts.

The four set off once more. Soon afterwards a violent storm broke, they got lost again and crossed the river without the slightest idea where they were going. They stopped near a scrap car dealer's to find out where they were. Some Alsatians were barking on the other side of the fence surrounding the scrap-yard, and when one of the dogs got out onto the road and went for them, the four got back into their car and made a getaway.

They followed a maintenance road that ran beside a long grey wall, and finally reached a barbed-wire fence. However, this consisted of rows of barbed-wire mounted on wooden trestles, and they couldn't find any holes to climb through.

They heard whistles, shouts, a shot fired in the air, and saw soldiers come running through the rain. Without noticing it, they had gone past a sign that said: CROSSING PROHIBITED — ARMY LAND. So they were on the run again, heading back towards the bridge over the big river.

Two days later, as they were going along the river embankment, they stole a tarpaulin from a motorboat moored to the bank and made for the mouth of the river with their friend wrapped in the tarpaulin on the car roof.

The countryside all around this area was pretty well uninhabited. Road signs gave the names of non-existent places, or rather, places where houses had been abandoned or knocked down, and where new houses built of concrete stood empty.

Along the sides of a field of maize they saw scarecrows made from plastic bottles stuck onto sticks and nylon bags that flapped in the wind.

Just beyond a crossroads, some young motorcyclists had stopped at a level-crossing — behind them a country road wound its way through the tall grass and a line of smoke-filled chimneys blocked the horizon. They wanted to ask them for information but, at the last minute, not one of the four dared open his mouth, and they stayed there at the level-crossing unable to decide. They were afraid of people hearing their voices and their accents, which didn't come from around there.

Stopping on a small road that ran down from the embankment, they contemplated a point out in the plain where a series of tracks crossed. Here the wheat had already been harvested and a stray combine was turning the hay into bales as it moved slowly forward. This is also the place from which they saw the big river full of refuse that floated motionless on the surface — there were white bubbles as if some setting agent had been dissolved in the water, causing the water to stagnate and turning it absolutely black, except for the white bubbles.

It was on this embankment that a knife-grinder came towards them. He used to go around on an old motorcycle with a sidecar, and had a loudspeaker for hailing the people living in the small, box-like houses that could be seen on the other side of the fields. The knife-grinder stopped and greeted them. He began to chatter away to himself, continually going off at a tangent, and he finally started speaking in dialect about an area called 'deadmen's sack', which, according to him, stretched into a lagoon about thirty kilometres from there.

The four came from a region a long way away and didn't understand the dialect spoken in these parts, so they couldn't really make out what the knife-grinder was saying. However, the name of the area stuck in their minds.

They were on a poorly tarred road in front of a villa complete with garden and gushing fountain, when they found themselves feeling thirsty. They hadn't managed to find a public fountain

anywhere and didn't dare go into a bar. So they went into the garden and were drinking from a jet of water, when an old man in underpants and slippers carrying a newspaper came into view and then ran and hid round a corner.
They ran round this corner and there was no one there. The air was thick with pollen and a voice inside the house began shouting: 'Help, thieves !'

The four of them began to tremble from head to foot. They got back into their car and drove off, and were still trembling an hour later.

Pressing on, they came across a lock and this is where the canals with their steep banks of reeds and bog grass began their long journey — they could see marshlands covered in moss in the far distance. Further on, an empty football field under an embankment caught their eye and they just couldn't stop staring at it. From the moment they had gone to live in the tile-manufacturing town, they had never set foot outside it, and everything about the places they were now passing through appeared unusual, out of the ordinary.

They would hear more of deadmen's sack (the area the knife-grinder had spoken of) that very night.

On the road that ran through the pitch-black countryside, they could see, on one side, the lights of the gas refinery dotted along a grid like some city in a lunar landscape, and, on the other, a green light in the distance that kept flashing on and off.

A man by the name of Mazinga had a caravan by the roadside in this part of the world and he sold sandwiches, soft drinks and ice cream to passers-by who had got lost among the lagoons. He called the place his 'airport', and that was the reason why he had installed a green flashing light on his caravan, like those used in airports for signalling.

On the run in the pitch-black countryside, the four realized that they were famished, for it was a long time since they had last eaten. Furthermore, after the frightening experience at the villa, all four of them often started trembling for no apparent reason, and that made them even more disoriented. So, in order to get their bearings, they followed the flashing green light and eventually arrived at Mazinga's airport.

They bought drinks and sandwiches at the caravan. After he had served them, the caravan man sat in a deckchair and watched television on a small portable set. He was a fat little man with a baseball cap on his head. A sign on the caravan said, in English, MAZINGA OPEN NIGHT AND DAY.

While they were standing eating their sandwiches, the four friends noticed that the caravan man was talking to himself as he watched television. Then they also noticed that it was them he was talking about as he mumbled to himself. He was mumbling to himself saying that they'd get them just like they got the others; that they'd be even more like the vile bastards they were with them, because they were innocent; that they'd either break them or turn them into murderous beasts like themselves; that that's how it is in this world, and there is no other world, and there can be no other, and it's no use hoping it were otherwise.

Perhaps the man had read about them in the papers. Anyway he knew all about them and kept mumbling these words to himself.

The four friends started trembling from head to foot once more. The youngest one's teeth were chattering so loudly that they made an echoing sound in the night, so that the caravan man turned around to see what was going on. He shook his head and went back to his television.

As he watched television, he said that the one and only way of getting to safety was to go to deadmen's sack — 'Only in deadmen's sack are you safe,' he said. Then he explained where it was, switched off the television, and, without glancing up, went off to bed.

The next day at about twelve o'clock, after they had been travelling around the delta in no obvious direction, the four stopped in a small village to find some road maps. They wanted to find the place the caravan-man had told them about.

Along a canal there were old, abandoned houses which had

once belonged to fishermen, and on the other side of the road there were new houses with washing on the line and lots of mopeds, bicycles and cars outside the front doors. Men in vests were washing their cars or smoking and chatting on the doorstep. From the windows came the sing-song of women talking, and in the open space in front of the houses the children seemed the only ones to notice their car as it passed.

In a bar crowded with men dressed in black, they looked around for someone to ask where they could find road maps. The woman who served behind the bar didn't undertand either the words they used or their accent, and went on shaking her head while serving other customers. None of the men standing at the bar showed any sign of acknowledging their presence. They were all busy discussing a political event reported in the newspaper, and one of them was waving the paper in the others' faces as he spoke.

Not far from the bar a coach drew up, full of tourists who were being taken to see the mouth of the big river. A guide harangued the visitors through a megaphone and his voice sounded full of fury.

All of a sudden the voice started to curse because an elderly woman felt unwell in the heat of the sun. And when the tourist fell to the ground, the voice shouted for her to be carried to the coach as there was no time to lose. Other tourists rushed forward yelling as though they were desperate, the coach driver blew his horn because he was in a hurry, and even some young lads on mopeds started blowing their horns all at once.

The four made off in a state of shock — they ran to their car and took flight yet again. By this time, the slightest thing frightened them, causing them to tremble from head to foot.

As they didn't have any road maps, they had no idea where to go. While they were driving blindly around, a stone punctured a tyre and they finished up in a ditch.

They abandoned their car. Carrying their dead friend with them, they set off again through the marshes and into areas of reeds and bog grass, beyond which there was only the sea. When they started feeling hungry again, they began to cry. They spent a whole day and a whole night sitting on the ground crying.

Still crying, they tried to follow paths that didn't exist and frequently sank into holes full of water or quicksands as they tramped on in search of something out in the lagoons. In the evening, cold and famished, they cried themselves to sleep and even carried on crying in their sleep.

One morning they woke up and realized that they had stopped crying, they had even stopped trembling. In front of them was a hut of corrugated iron with a roof made of reinforced asbestos. It was the place Mazinga had told them about.

In the hut were the remains of a snack that someone must have suddenly interrupted many many years earlier. The blankets on the two camp beds, eaten away by time, had become a thick layer of dust. A number of mosquitoes filled the air with their humming, and outside the door could be seen a boat that was moored to a pier of black, rotting planks which was surrounded by reeds.

They went well out to sea in that boat and let their dead friend slide into the water. Afterwards they didn't know how to decide when to turn back and went on rowing. They had the idea in their heads that, if they went on rowing, they would reach some place or other.